NOWHERE TO RUN

"Check over there!" someone yelled. "She couldn't have gotten out of here yet."

Her heart racing, Lisa quickly considered her options. *If I can get them to follow me,* she thought, *maybe I can circle around them farther ahead.* At that moment there was a shout and one of the men pointed in her direction. Without hesitation she whirled Stewball around and urged him into a mad gallop.

Lisa didn't dare look back—it was taking every last ounce of concentration simply to stay in the saddle. The path she had chosen was getting narrower and narrower, and, to her dismay, there was a steep drop on either side of her. Any hopes she'd harbored about slipping off onto a side trail were dashed.

"Give it up, little girl," one of the men called. "There's nowhere to go from there. It's a dead end."

"Leave me alone!" Lisa screamed.

Then, to her complete horror, she felt Stewball lurch beneath her, and the two of them went over the cliff.

the SADDLE CLUB

TRAIL RIDE

BONNIE BRYANT

A SKYLARK BOOK

NEW YORK • TORONTO • LONDON • SYDNEY • AUCKLAND

RL 3.6, AGES 008–012

TRAIL RIDE
A Bantam Skylark Book / July 2001

ISBN: 0-553-48741-8

Published simultaneously in the United States and Canada

Bantam Skylark is an imprint of Random House Children's Books.
SKYLARK BOOK, BANTAM BOOKS, and the rooster colophon
are registered trademarks of Random House, Inc. Bantam Books,
1540 Broadway, New York, New York 10036.

PRINTED IN THE UNITED STATES OF AMERICA
OPM   10 9 8 7 6 5 4 3 2

My special thanks to Cat Johnston
for her help in the writing of this book.

Thanks also to Peter J. Zeale, M.D.,
and Mary Kay Tobin, M.D.,
for their expertise.

"ONLY ONE MONTH of summer left," Stevie Lake said, thumping her empty lemonade glass down on the dresser. "We have to wring maximum yield from it."

Carole Hanson, sprawled lazily across the bed, exchanged looks of amusement with their other friend, Lisa Atwood, who was curled up in the window seat. " 'Maximum yield,' Stevie? You and your brothers weren't by any chance watching the Sci-Fi Channel last night while your parents were out, were you?"

"The forbidden Sci-Fi Channel?" Lisa asked, raising her eyebrows inquiringly.

"I refuse to answer on the grounds that I might incriminate myself," Stevie told them airily.

Carole laughed and rolled onto her back. "Spoken like the true daughter of two attorneys."

"Besides"—Stevie grinned—"it was the original black-and-white version of *The Thing*."

"Oh yeah, the carrot creature," Carole murmured. "My dad really likes that one."

"Excuse me?" Lisa said from her sunny perch. "The *carrot* creature?"

"A space alien frozen in the ice of Alaska," Stevie told her.

"Antarctica," Carole corrected.

"Whatever. Anyway, they thaw it out and it begins killing all the scientists."

Carole nodded. "Yeah, that about covers it."

"Wait a minute. Where does the carrot part come in?" Lisa asked, confused.

"The alien is carrot-shaped," Stevie said impatiently. "I can't believe you haven't seen this movie."

"Yeah," Carole said, resting her chin on her hand. "My dad probably has a book on the making of it somewhere in his library."

Lisa rose lazily to her feet and stretched. "That's because your dad loves any movie made in black and white."

Carole sat up. "Hey! Dad is very discriminating."

"Let me get this straight," Lisa said, crossing her arms. "The movie is about a giant frozen carrot from outer space that successfully terrorizes and kills Earth's most intelligent scientists."

"You're oversimplifying," Carole told her.

Stevie grinned. "No, actually, she's not. At least, not from what I saw last night."

"Very sophisticated stuff," Lisa said, giggling.

Carole tossed a small heart-shaped pillow at her. "All right, that's enough. I thought we were going to have a meeting of The Saddle Club."

"I thought we were in the middle of one already," Stevie said.

"That's the trouble with The Saddle Club." Lisa sighed. "We're so fly-by-the-seat-of-our-pants."

Stevie frowned. "What do you mean? We have regular meetings."

"We don't even have a president!" Lisa pointed out. "Let alone a vice president or secretary."

"There are only three of us in the entire club," Carole reminded her. "We would each have to take two titles simply to fill out a proper roster, and then there would be no one left for us to boss around."

"Could I be treasurer?" Stevie asked brightly.

"No!" Carole and Lisa responded firmly.

3

"Killjoys."

"At least we have rules," Carole pointed out.

"Two! We have two whole rules," Lisa said. "What kind of club has only two rules?"

Carole shrugged. "I think they're very good rules, as rules go."

Stevie pulled herself to attention and placed one hand on her heart. "Rule number one: You must be crazy about horses."

Carole climbed to her feet and also placed her hand on her heart solemnly. "Rule number two: You must be willing to help the other members out, no matter what." She nudged Stevie in the ribs. "By the way I think you're abusing that one."

Stevie's mouth dropped open, and she put her hands on her hips. "It's not my fault!"

Lisa and Carole both gave her a *tell us another one* look.

"Things just happen to me!"

"Stevie," Lisa said, "if you spent half as much time riding as you do playing practical jokes on people, you'd probably be the youngest equestrian Olympian by now."

"And if Lisa and I didn't have to spend half our time trying to figure out how to get you out of hot water, she

4

could have graduated early and I would have been in veterinary school already," added Carole.

"Oh, you've decided, then?" Lisa said, turning to her friend with great interest.

"No, I still don't now exactly what I want to do when I get older, but . . ."

"It's definitely going to have to do with horses," Stevie and Lisa finished together.

Lisa sighed wistfully. "When we formed The Saddle Club, I kind of thought we might end up with more members."

Stevie found Lisa's attitude annoying. The Saddle Club was the center of her universe. There was nothing she wouldn't do for her two best friends, or they for her. "We do have more members," she argued. "It's just that they're absentee members. Anyway, look at all the adventures we've shared."

"Remember making that movie with Skye Ransom?" Carole asked.

Lisa got a dreamy look on her face. Skye was a well-known actor whom The Saddle Club had helped teach how to ride for one of his movies. Lisa had definitely had a crush on him.

"Who put a burr under your saddle anyhow?" Stevie asked Lisa.

Her friend shrugged. "I don't know. It's something my mom said about time slipping away without people noticing. I guess it got me thinking."

Stevie was determined to bring the subject of the remaining days of summer back into focus. "Speaking of time, we only have a few weeks of summer left. What are we going to do with them?"

"I really want to work with Starlight on dressage techniques," Carole declared. "A horse well trained in dressage moves so precisely, it's really beautiful to watch. Like you and Belle, Stevie."

Stevie blushed at the compliment. She knew she was one of the best dressage riders at Pine Hollow Stables, but to have someone as knowledgeable as Carole say so was a great pat on the back. "Thanks, Carole. I'd be glad to give you pointers anytime."

"Yeah, I know. That's why I was buttering you up."

Stevie playfully shoved Carole, who fell back on to the bed, laughing. "Okay, then," she retorted, "you have to work with Belle and me on jumping. It's only fair."

"Sure. Happy to do it."

Stevie crouched at nose level with her friend. "We'll see how happy you are when Belle and I snatch that blue ribbon out from under you at the next horse show."

"In your dreams."

"What about me?" Lisa asked.

Stevie felt a twinge of guilt. Lisa was the newest of the three to riding. She was doing fantastically well—a real natural—but she relied on Stevie and Carole for reassurance and guidance. "You're going to be working with Prancer, right?" Stevie asked.

Lisa nodded. Unlike her two friends, she didn't have her own horse yet. But Max Regnery, who owned the stables where the three of them rode, let her use a wonderful horse named Prancer on a regular basis. She was a former racehorse and tended to be a bit high-strung. "Any suggestions?"

"Prancer's still kind of jumpy," Stevie noted.

"What about some intensive trail riding?" Carole asked.

Lisa shrugged. "We've done that before. What would be the point? Outside of having a nice day of riding, I mean."

Carole smiled thoughtfully. "I was thinking more along the line of a guerrilla trail ride."

Stevie perked up. "Tricks and traps?" she said eagerly.

"What are you two talking about?"

Stevie grinned. "Carole and I would set up a series of minor events."

"You know, a piece of paper blown across the trail, a sudden car horn going off, that kind of thing," Carole explained.

"You'd know all about it beforehand," Stevie said, winking. "But Prancer wouldn't."

"I get it. It might help her with shying and overreacting."

Carole cut in. "And since you would know ahead of time what was coming, it wouldn't be dangerous for you."

"Prancer would start getting used to the unexpected and come to rely on her amazingly unflappable rider," Stevie finished with a flourish.

"That would really boost her confidence in me!" Lisa said enthusiastically.

"And yours in her," Carole added wisely.

A knock on the bedroom door interrupted them.

"Carole?"

"Yeah, Dad, come on in," she called cheerfully.

Colonel Hanson opened the door.

"Hi, Colonel Hanson," Stevie said brightly. Carole's dad was one of her favorite adults. "Heard any good jokes lately?"

"Not one," the colonel said, shaking his head gloomily. "But I've got a couple of really bad ones," he added, breaking into a conspiratorial grin.

Stevie clapped her hands together in approval. "Excellent!" The two of them shared a love for the kind of jokes that would make most people groan at the punch line.

"Stop by the kitchen on your way home and I'll share them with you."

"You got it," Stevie agreed happily.

"Meanwhile, my darling daughter," he informed Carole. "The phone is for you."

They all looked at each other. Who could it be? They were all there.

"Who is it, Dad?"

"Long distance from the Wild West," he informed her.

Carole jumped to her feet. "Kate?"

"Affirmative. Why don't you three take it in the den. You can use the speakerphone."

The girls almost knocked the colonel down in their rush to get downstairs.

"Thanks, Dad!" Carole called over her shoulder.

Her dad chuckled good-naturedly. "No problem, hon."

"Hah! Another member of The Saddle Club," Stevie crowed triumphantly as she raced down the hall in pursuit of Carole.

"All right," Lisa laughed. "I guess we do have more than three members."

Kate Devine was one of the out-of-town members of The Saddle Club. She lived out West with her mom and dad on a dude ranch called the Bar None. She was a kindred spirit and the girls visited her as often as they could, learning how to ride Western and relishing the wide-open spaces.

Carole punched a button on the speakerphone. "Kate? Are you there?"

"Hi, Carole," Kate said, her voice coming through loud and clear. "How are things?"

"Terrific," Carole told her. "Your timing is great. Guess who's standing right beside me?"

"Lisa and Stevie?"

"Hi, Kate," the two of them chorused.

"Are you calling from the Bar None?" Carole asked.

"Where else?"

"Are you coming out here to visit by any chance?" Lisa asked hopefully.

"No-o-o."

"Rats!" Stevie said, scowling. "We could use some new blood around here."

"Summer boredom setting in, Stevie?" Kate chuckled.

"Well, maybe a little."

"Good," Kate told her. "Then you won't mind taking a little break from the city life. Christine had to go out of town to visit her grandparents, and I could really use some company."

A trill of excitement ran through the girls.

Stevie held up five fingers and waved them under Lisa's nose. "That's five," she said triumphantly. Christine Lonetree was also a member of The Saddle Club. She lived close to Kate and was every bit as horse-crazy as the others. She was also a Native American Indian and had taught the other girls a lot about her culture and heritage.

"Okay, already. I get the point," Lisa laughed.

Carole waved at them to be quiet. "Kate, are you saying what I think you're saying?"

"Yep. My dad has to fly a corporate client to Washington next week, and since the plane will be empty on the return trip, he got permission to pick you all up and bring you back here with him. Then he can return you when he goes to pick the guy up again."

For a moment the room reverberated with the sound of excited squeals of joy.

"I'll take that as a yes," Kate said when the noise had died down enough for her to make herself heard.

"Will we!" Stevie crowed. "We wouldn't miss it for the world!"

"Of course, we'll have to check with our parents first," Carole reminded them.

"Your dad already said it was okay," Kate informed her joyfully.

"I'm sure my parents won't mind. They'll also be glad to get rid of me for a while," Stevie said.

"Hey! My dad doesn't want to get rid of me," Carole said indignantly.

Stevie rolled her eyes. "You know what I mean."

Carole grinned. "Just giving you a hard time."

"So what else is new?" Kate laughed. "How about you, Lisa? Do you think you can make it?"

"I don't see why not," she said slowly. "My dad's out of town again. I'm sure Mom won't mind having the house all to herself."

"Terrific! Call me back when you know for sure. I can't wait to see you."

"Same here," the three of them said in unison.

"Talk to you soon."

"Bye." Carole hung up.

"We're going out West!" Stevie hollered, dancing around the room with joy. "Yahoo!"

"Make that *yee haw!*" Carole countered, dancing with her.

"Wait a minute!" Lisa yelled over the two of them. "Some of us haven't checked with our folks yet."

Stevie stopped dancing. "Ah, the voice of reason rears its ugly head."

"Who are you calling ugly?"

"You, if you don't stop raining on the parade," Stevie told her. "We're a shoo-in."

Lisa sniffed. "I just don't think we should count our chickens before they hatch, that's all."

"She's right," Carole concurred. "Why don't you both call your parents right now so we can celebrate properly."

"Good idea, Carole," Stevie said. "I'll go first." She turned to the phone, but Lisa was already holding it.

"Hi, Mom," Lisa said, sticking her tongue out at Stevie.

Outmaneuvered, Stevie thought, pacing impatiently while Lisa explained things to her mom.

Since Lisa wasn't using the speaker option, Stevie and Carole could only hear one side of the conversation.

"We were all invited," Lisa was saying into the phone. "No, Stevie hasn't asked yet, but she doesn't think it will be a problem, and Colonel Hanson has already said that Carole can go." She listened for a moment. "Yeah, Mom, the Bar None. I know we haven't returned their hospitality from the last time, but it's okay. They don't care about stuff like that."

Carole and Stevie exchanged glances. Lisa's mother was a stickler for good manners. Sometimes they thought Mrs. Atwood was a little too worried about social appearances. In fact, they suspected the reason she had let Lisa start riding in the first place was that Mrs. diAngelo, the leading socialite in town, had had her daughter enrolled in riding classes at Pine Hollow.

"No, Mom, I don't need any new clothes," Lisa said, rolling her eyes at her friends. "I can wear whatever." She paused, then sighed heavily. "Okay, okay, we can go shopping tomorrow if you want." She listened again. "I know you'll be alone, but I thought you liked that once in a while."

Stevie crossed her fingers. It sounded like Lisa was winning the case. She sure hoped so, because it wouldn't be the same going to the Bar None without the entire Saddle Club.

"Okay, Mom, I'll be home in a little while. Bye." Lisa hung up. She looked troubled.

"Well?" Stevie demanded.

"I can go," Lisa told them quietly.

"Yay!" Carole and Stevie danced around the room again, but when Lisa didn't join in, they stopped.

"What's wrong?" Carole asked. "Aren't you happy?"

"Of course I am," Lisa assured her. "Only . . ."

"What?" Stevie asked.

"I don't know. Mom sounded kind of . . . weird."

Carole perched on the edge of her dad's desk. "Weird how?"

Lisa shrugged. "She sounded kind of lonely."

"You said your dad's out of town again, right?"

Lisa nodded. "He's been gone a lot lately. Even more than usual."

"Don't worry, Lisa. As soon as he comes home, your mom will be fine," Carole reassured her.

"And you'll be out West!" added Stevie. She grabbed the phone and started dialing.

Lisa brightened visibly. "You guys are right." She pulled a sour face. "Of course I have to get a whole new wardrobe."

"You know, some girls would enjoy that," Carole reminded her.

"I know, but lately all my mom wants to do is shop, shop, shop."

"Quiet, everybody!" Stevie whispered sharply.

Lisa and Carole gave her affronted looks.

15

"My mom's at the office, so shush." She turned her attention to the phone and said brightly, "Hi, Mrs. Renfrew, it's Stevie. How are you? I'm great, thanks for asking. How are your boys?"

Lisa and Carole began to snicker.

Stevie, who was doing her best to maintain a polite conversation with her mother's secretary, waved them away. "Is Mom there?" she asked sweetly. "Thanks." She shot a baleful look at Lisa and Carole.

When Mrs. Lake got on the phone, Stevie gleefully filled her in on the exciting events and waited expectantly. There was a long pause. "What?" she shrieked. "You're kidding! *No-o-o-o-o!*" Stevie threw herself into Colonel Hanson's swivel chair. "I totally blacked it out."

Carole and Lisa exchanged concerned looks.

"Aww, come on, Mom, nobody would miss me," Stevie coaxed. "It's not like I'm one of the bridesmaids!" She swiveled furiously in the chair. "Besides, according to statistics, she'll probably be getting married again, anyway. I can go next time."

Mrs. Lake's response could be heard all the way across the room. Lisa and Carole cringed.

"Sorry, Mom," Stevie said contritely. "I'm sure it's a match made in heaven." She mimed sticking her finger down her throat at her two friends. "No, Mother, I did not just make a face."

Carole and Lisa put their hands over their mouths in an attempt to smother their laughter.

"But I won't have anyone to talk to," Stevie wailed. "Who?" she demanded, jumping to her feet. "Cousin Dava? Mom, have you lost it? She hates everything, even horses!"

Stevie spent the next few minutes arguing hotly with her mother, but it was obviously no use. Finally she hung up and sat glowering at the phone.

"Problem?" Carole said after a minute.

"I can't go!" Stevie told them, near tears. "My cousin is getting married and Mom says the whole family has to be there to support her." She thumped her head onto the desk. "I hate my cousins!" she said passionately.

"Stevie, you know that's not true," Lisa said in a shocked tone.

Stevie looked up. "Okay, I just hate my cousin Dava."

"That's more like it," Carole said.

Bad as she felt, Stevie couldn't help venting a little. "You know, if I had another week, I could figure out how to get out of this."

Lisa put a consoling arm around her shoulders. "I don't doubt that for a minute."

Stevie pulled herself together. "On the bright side, Mom said I could use her new Quicky-Mail thingy to send messages to you guys any time I wanted."

"Oh, I've heard about those things," Lisa cooed. "It's one of those wireless miniature computers that you can use to send and receive e-mail. All you have to do is hold it in front of the mouthpiece."

"Very cool," Carole concurred.

"I can't believe this is happening to me," Stevie said glumly. "You guys have to promise to write me every single day and give me all the details!"

"We promise," Lisa assured her.

"I bet it won't be nearly as much fun as we think it will be," Carole told her stoutly.

"Oh be quiet, Sally Sunshine," Stevie snapped. She sat back and surveyed her two best friends. They were obviously excited to be going and almost as upset as she was that she couldn't be there as well. "Well," she said, "at least it'll be happy trails for some of The Saddle Club."

CAROLE AND LISA stood by the gate to the runway, clutching their suitcases expectantly.

"Have you ever seen Stevie looking so down?" Lisa murmured.

"Not often," Carole admitted.

"She couldn't even come and see us off."

"I know. When she drove away this morning, she looked like she was going to her own execution."

"Can't blame her. No trip to the Bar None, no Saddle Club meetings, no riding."

The two girls shuddered at the very thought.

"Do they even have horses where she's going?" Lisa asked.

"In Massachusetts? Of course they do!" Carole said. "At least I think they do."

"No electricity, though," Colonel Hanson said quietly.

"Dad! Stop that."

"Come on, you two, cheer up. Stevie is going to be fine. She always manages to land on her feet."

"Maybe she'll even find a way to ride," Lisa said hopefully.

"She did take along her riding stuff," Carole whispered.

"How'd she manage to get that past her mom?"

"She stuffed it in with the spare tire last night while she was supposed to be doing the dishes," Carole told her, grinning.

Lisa chuckled. "That's our Stevie."

"There's your ride, girls," Colonel Hanson said, pointing to a sleek white-and-blue jet descending toward the runway. It touched down with barely a bump and taxied over to the gate where they were waiting.

Carole felt her heart start to race with excitement. She was devastated that Stevie wouldn't be with them for the trip, but she was sure glad she was going anyway.

The aircraft came to a complete stop and after a few minutes the door was opened, unfolding into a set of stairs. A bright strip of red carpeting rolled down, shooting across the pavement toward them.

Colonel Hanson laughed. "Looks like you girls are getting the red-carpet treatment," he said with raised eyebrows.

Carole and Lisa exchanged excited looks.

A man appeared in the doorway of the plane and waved at the three of them.

"Frank!" Colonel Hanson called, striding forward.

Frank Devine trotted down the steps and met him halfway. "Mitch! You old warhorse." The girls watched as the two men shook hands and slapped each other on the back with obvious delight.

Lisa looked at Carole. "Old warhorse?"

"It's a military thing," she giggled. "Hi, Mr. Devine."

"Carole! Lisa!" He swooped them both up in a bear hug.

"Nice uniform, Mr. Devine," Lisa told him once she had been released.

"You like?" He straightened his navy blue tie. "My official flying togs. I just dropped the boss off in D.C. Very important banking business." He winked. "Now I'm all yours. You girls ready to go?"

"We can't wait," Carole said happily. "How are Kate and Mrs. Devine?"

21

"Terrific," he assured them. "But you can judge for yourself in a few hours."

"I think that's your cue to get on board, girls," Colonel Hanson said.

"Yep, we're burning daylight," Mr. Devine told them, rubbing his hands together.

Carole remembered that *burning daylight* was an old Western term. Cowboys had to get up at the crack of dawn in order to get all their work done before the sun went down. She felt a shiver of anticipation run down her spine. "Ready when you are, sir," she said, saluting him smartly.

Mr. Devine laughed and saluted her back. "She's a chip off the old block, Mitch."

Carole's dad looked pleased. "You take care of my girls now, Frank. Have fun, sweetheart," he said, giving Carole a big hug. "Stay out of trouble."

"Sure thing, Dad," she murmured, returning the embrace. For a moment she thought she might cry. Ever since her mother had died, Carole had found it difficult leaving her dad alone. She gave herself a mental shake, kissed him on the cheek, and headed for the plane.

"A red carpet, Mr. Devine?" Lisa said, stepping gingerly on the plush material.

"Nothing but the best for you two," he told them, striding up the stairs. "The most spectacular views, the richest caviar, the most expensive champagne." He turned around to face them. "You did bring your fake IDs, right?"

Lisa laughed. "Mr. Devine!"

Chuckling, he led the way inside.

The interior of the plane was lavish. Carole and Lisa had both been on commercial airlines before, passing through first class on their way to economy seating, but this was something truly special. The compact interior appeared remarkably spacious, because instead of rows and rows of seats jammed together, there were only a few huge reclining chairs upholstered in dove gray leather. A handful of low smoky glass tables were bolted to the floor, and the windows had curtains in a shade of burgundy that complemented the chairs and pearl carpeting perfectly.

"Good morning, ladies. Welcome aboard."

The girls turned to see a pretty young woman, immaculately dressed in a tailored uniform, smiling at them.

"Girls, allow me to introduce Ms. Penny Jane Minns, flight attendant extraordinaire."

"Oh, Frank, go fly the plane or you'll make me

blush," the woman said good-naturedly. "You must be Lisa and Carole," she said, shaking hands with them in the right order. "You can call me Penny."

"How did you know who's name was which?" Lisa asked.

"Frank told me a lot about you girls. A *lot*," she emphasized.

Carole felt herself blush. "Sorry."

Penny laughed. "Don't be. Your adventures would make a good book or two." She escorted them to their chairs. "Let's get you buckled in for takeoff."

She watched as they adjusted their seat belts, then gave them each a fluffy pillow.

"It's going to take a few more minutes until we're cleared for takeoff. Why don't I get you a drink in the meantime? A little bubbly okay?" She held up a ginger ale bottle with a smile.

"Thank you very much," they said happily.

While Penny was pouring their drinks, Lisa turned to Carole. "Look at these pillows," she whispered, clutching hers in her lap. "It's real linen, not that disposable paper stuff they use on regular airlines! I wonder what the thread count is?"

Carole could hardly believe her ears. *Thread count?* "You know, Lisa, this vacation from your mother might be exactly what the doctor ordered, because I think you're losing it."

Penny returned a moment later with two crystal champagne flutes filled with "bubbly." Carole had never felt so sophisticated.

Minutes after they had finished their drinks, the private plane taxied down the runway and rose gently into the air.

"I wish Stevie were here," Lisa said, pushing a button to recline her chair. "Whoa!" The seat back fell away, a footrest flew up, and she found herself lying on a bed.

Carole burst into laughter and reclined her chair as well. "It doesn't seem right without her. We'll have to be sure to e-mail her every single day and tell her what a miserable time we're having."

"Right," Lisa said, popping a macadamia nut into her mouth. "Miserable."

Penny appeared in the aisle next to them. "Now that we're under way, I can start serving lunch," she told them. "While I'm getting it ready, I thought you might like to watch some TV." She punched a button and a large screen rolled down the wall. "If you can't find anything you like, we also have an extensive video library on board. There's a list in the side pocket of your seats."

The two girls straightened up their chairs and pulled out the multipage list.

"If you don't both want to watch the same program, there are individual screens that unfold from under the seats," she said helpfully.

"Thank you," Carole said with a grin. "I'm sure this will be fine."

"I'll be back in a second with your appetizers."

Lisa turned to Carole. "Appetizers? We get appetizers?"

Carole almost guffawed. "I'd ask you to pinch me," she said, "but our seats are too far apart."

Lisa pointed her nose in the air. "After all, this is first class, my dear," she drawled.

Penny returned and unfolded hidden tray tables in each of the girls' armrests. The girls watched in fascination as she placed real silverware, linen napkins, place mats, and individual crystal salt and pepper shakers on each of their tables.

"Look at that!" exclaimed Lisa. "No plastic forks or little paper packets."

Shortly after, Penny presented them with silver servers of shrimp cocktail: large shrimp nestled on beds of crisp iceberg lettuce and smothered in zesty red sauce. "Bon appétit, ladies," she said as she departed.

Lisa looked down at her appetizer. "What, no oyster crackers? What kind of joint are they running here?"

Before they could even laugh, Penny swept back in

carrying individual china dishes of crackers. "The adults don't usually go for these, but it may help to wash the fishy stuff down."

"Th-Thank you," Lisa stammered.

"By the way, I didn't have time to make the usual lobster Thermidor," she said apologetically. "I hope you two won't mind burgers and fries for the main course?"

Lisa and Carole beamed their approval.

"Didn't think so," she chuckled, heading back to the galley.

Lunch concluded with ice cream sundaes with a choice of toppings, which reminded Carole and Lisa once again of Stevie.

"Can you imagine what kind of sundae Stevie would have ordered?" Carole asked.

"Pistachio ice cream with pineapple sauce?"

"And grape jelly."

"And cherries or banana chips."

Both girls burst into laughter at the thought.

Stevie's sundaes were the stuff of legend: any and every topping, the weirder the combination the better. Her friends were convinced she only did it so that nobody would ask her for a taste, but still, it was uniquely Stevie.

"I'm so miserable," Carole moaned, licking the last of her fudge topping from her spoon.

"Are you insane?" Lisa demanded, wiping her mouth on her linen napkin.

"No, I'm practicing for Stevie. Do I sound convincing?"

"Sorry, I don't see an Academy Award in your future. But I really do miss her."

"Me too."

"After-lunch mint?" Penny said brightly.

"If you insist," Lisa said cheerfully.

"Good idea." Carole smiled. "After all, I wouldn't want to offend anybody with my chocolate breath."

The rest of the flight passed quickly and smoothly with the help of the plane's video library. Almost before they knew it, Penny was telling them to return their seats to the upright position in preparation for landing.

When Carole saw the airport near Two Mile Creek come into view, she felt her pulse begin to race. "Betcha I can spot Kate first from up here," she challenged Lisa.

"No way," Lisa responded, pressing her face against her window. "Not without your Seeing Eye dog."

Carole laughed and returned to scanning the ground below.

28

"There they are!" Lisa cried a few minutes later. "I'd know that old truck anywhere."

Lisa was right. Carole could just make out the familiar pickup parked by the edge of the runway. Two small figures stood next to it, waving. She waved back, even though she was fairly certain she couldn't be seen yet.

The plane touched down gently and slowed to a stop. Minutes later Mr. Devine stepped out of the cockpit. "All ashore who's going ashore."

"Isn't that what they say on ships?" Lisa asked as she unbuckled and scrambled out of her seat.

"Never argue with the captain, young lady. Did you know I could have you keelhauled with the slightest wave of my pinkie?"

"No way, Mr. Devine," said Carole. "That's also for ships, not airplanes." She checked around her seat to make sure she hadn't forgotten anything.

"Mutiny! Penny, were having a mutiny!" Mr. Devine cried. "Lower the plank!" He opened the door and unfolded the steps. "Throw these two off my ship!"

"Plane!" Carole and Lisa said in unison.

Penny stepped in front of Mr. Devine and pretended to hold him back. "I think you girls had better make a run for it. He didn't get his medication today."

Laughing, they slid past her and through the

doorway. "Thanks for everything, Penny," Carole said. "It was fantastic!"

"You're the best," Lisa concurred.

Penny smiled. "Have a nice holiday, girls. I'll catch you on the flip side." She turned to Mr. Devine. "I love these deadheads." She disappeared into the cabin.

Lisa and Carole exchanged glances. "Deadheads?" they both protested.

A burst of laughter came from behind them. "Relax. A *deadhead* is what we call a trip without paying passengers."

"Oh," said Carole. "For a moment—" But her words were cut off as Kate and her mother ran over, and she found herself happily squashed in a group of overjoyed females. Hugs were coming from all sides, and she was determined to give as good as she was getting.

"Look how you've grown!" Mrs. Devine gushed, holding Lisa at arm's length. "Pretty soon you'll be taller than me."

"More of me to hug?" suggested Lisa.

Mrs. Devine laughed and swept her back into her arms. "Yes, dear, more of you to hug."

The three girls laughed.

"I can't believe you're finally here," Kate cried, holding their hands. "I thought last night was never going to end."

Carole could feel herself grinning like a maniac but felt helpless to stop it. "I know what you mean. I don't think I slept a wink all night."

Mrs. Devine seemed concerned. "Did you get a nap on the plane?"

From the corner of her eye, Carole saw Mr. Devine approaching. "Not a chance. The pilot is a real maniac."

Lisa nodded. "I was scared to shut my eyes for a second."

"I heard that!" Mr. Devine thundered from behind them. Carole and Lisa laughed with delight and pretended to seek refuge behind his wife and daughter. "Just for that, I'm going to carry these suitcases only as far as the truck. When you get to the ranch, it's everyone for herself." He plunked the girls' luggage into the back of the waiting truck. "So there."

"Isn't your dad coming with us?" Lisa asked.

Kate shook her head, causing her long ginger ponytail to swish gently back and forth. "Naw, he'll have to stick around for a while to do some routine maintenance. He's got his own car here, though, so we don't have to wait."

So saying, the girls piled into the bed of the pickup for the ride back to the Bar None Ranch. Once they had left the general area of the airport, the road quickly deteriorated into unpaved dirt, solidly packed but definitely bumpy. Occasionally they hit a particularly deep pit and the girls would be thrown together. After a couple of times they all started exaggerating the motions and began pitching themselves at each other, laughing and screeching.

Finally they settled back down.

"I wish Stevie could have come," Kate said, wiping a tear of laughter from her eye. "Some part of me still believes she's going to show up somehow."

"You wouldn't if you had seen how determined her mother looked when they drove off this morning," Lisa told her.

Carole felt her spirits dip a little. "Did you see how she was clutching that e-mail thingy to her chest like it was her only lifeline?"

"So what's the plan?" Kate asked. "How are we going to cheer her up?"

Carole shrugged. "We promised to e-mail her every single day, but now I'm not so sure that's a good idea."

Her two friends looked astonished. "Why not?" Lisa demanded.

"Think about it. When you're absolutely miserable,

the *last* thing you want to hear about is what a fabulous time your friends are having without you."

Kate nodded. "Misery loves company."

"Exactly."

"So you think we should tell her we're bored and not having any fun?" Lisa asked doubtfully. "Won't that be lying?"

"Think of it as exaggerating the low points," Carole told her. "We could say things like, the plane ride was long . . . and the turbulence wasn't *too* bad."

They passed under a large sign that announced their arrival at the Bar None Ranch.

"How about: The dirt road to the ranch seemed even bumpier and dustier than we remembered," Lisa suggested.

Kate looked insulted. "Hey!"

Lisa laughed. "I'm only doing what you and Carole told me to."

Kate shook her head. "I think this exaggerating thing is going to need some fine-tuning," she muttered.

The truck rolled to a stop in front of a sprawling ranch house, the front of which was encompassed by a spacious wooden porch scattered with comfortable-looking chairs. A large metal triangle, used to call everyone to meals, was hanging next to the front door. Arranged in a semicircle behind the main house were the guest bunkhouses and the barn.

"I put the three of you in your usual bunkhouse," Mrs. Devine said, opening the tailgate for the girls. Kate, could you take them inside and help them unpack? I have to check on dinner." She strode away.

The girls hauled their suitcases out of the bed of the pickup and followed Kate toward the wooden building. "I hope you guys are hungry, because Mom's been cooking all day for you."

Carole and Lisa exchanged glances behind her back. The truth was they had snacked and drank their way across the country on the plane. "Er . . . I could eat a horse," Carole told her.

Kate faced her, looking very solemn. "You know, that thar's a hanging offense in this here part of the country." She laughed. "Besides, Mom only slaughtered you a steer each. I, on the other hand, have peeled and mashed enough potatoes to feed half the county. Then there's the corn on the cob, the fresh baked bread with homemade jam, and Mom's world-class apple pie to be washed down with giant scoops of vanilla ice cream."

The three of them entered the warm confines of the bunkhouse. It was clear that Mrs. Devine had gone out of her way to make the place even more hospitable than it normally was. Along with the usual beds and familiar potbellied stove, there were fresh flowers and homemade cookies on each of the girls' nightstands and extra pillows with hand-embroidered cases on all three bunks. Huge, fluffy comforters completed the picture.

Kate threw herself down on one of the beds. "Oh. Mom left you each a little welcome-back-to-the-ranch gift under your pillows. And if the sheets smell a little funny, its because she insisted on putting some French powder between them to make sure they wouldn't smell musty." She grinned at her two friends. "So, we have a few minutes, what do you say to knocking out that desperately bored and unhappy e-mail to Stevie?"

Carole looked around her helplessly and inhaled a big breath. The smell of fragrant cooking was wafting over from the main house. "Hoo boy, you guys," she said seriously, "I think we're in trouble already."

35

LISA'S EYES POPPED open, and for a moment she was disoriented—until a crowing rooster announced the early hour and the previous day's events came flooding back to her. After a glorious flight, she and Carole were at the Bar None Ranch.

She looked around at the bunkhouse, allowing herself a few moments of utter peace, indulging in nothing more cerebral than watching small dust motes dance in the early morning light streaming through the windows. She wriggled her toes under the fluffy covers and pulled cool, crisp, country air into her lungs. She made a mental note to store up these memories to savor again during the grind of the upcoming school year.

"Good morning, Nightmare," she said to the little stuffed pony sitting on the pillow next to her head. It was the welcome-back gift Mrs. Devine had left for her. The little brown-and-white-striped, loosely stuffed, pony-shaped bag was filled with peppermint and chamomile and was meant to be placed soothingly across the eyes or forehead. Carole had received a similar bag, which she had named Glory, after a foal she had helped birth.

Looking to her right, Lisa saw that Carole was not only still asleep but had apparently decided that plastering Glory over her eyes was the best response to the bright sunshine and rowdy rooster's chorus. Lisa rolled over to check on Kate. To her surprise the bed was not only empty, it was made!

Lisa sat up abruptly. The air that had seemed so crisp and refreshing moments before suddenly felt chilly and uninviting. She yanked the covers up over her pajama top and forced herself into full wakefulness.

Of course Kate's up and gone, she thought. *This is a dude ranch and everybody has morning chores*. A wave of guilt washed over her for her lazy city ways. She leaned over the side of her bed and spotted her new slippers. Wrinkling her nose distastefully, she picked one up. The red velvet monstrosities had her initials monogrammed on

37

the toes in gold thread: her mother's idea of what the "best people wore." She hated them. Taking careful aim, she tossed one at Carole's feet.

Carole muttered and rolled over, pulling her feet far under the covers, unknowingly presenting Lisa with her pajama-clad backside as a target.

"Wakey, wakey," Lisa called sweetly.

Carole's response was muffled by her pillow, but Lisa was fairly sure she had said something along the lines of "Just five more minutes, Dad."

Unable to resist the target, Lisa lobbed her other slipper at Carole's defenseless posterior. She was delighted with her accuracy and the groan from her victim. "Rise and shine!" she bellowed.

Carole faced her in a flash, sitting up stiffly and planting both bare feet firmly on the cold wood planking. "Lisa!" she cried with outrage. "I was still sleeping."

"Oooh, looks like somebody's not a morning person," said a voice from the doorway. Kate strolled in, carrying a tray.

Carole rubbed her hands over her face. "Morning, Kate. Thanks, Lisa," she added sheepishly. "I might have slept the whole morning away."

"Jet lag?" Kate inquired sympathetically. "A lot of our greenhorns experience that."

Lisa felt herself bristle and then realized their friend was merely teasing them. "I'm exhausted," she said, throwing herself back on the pillow melodramatically. "What's that? Room service?"

Kate gave her a baleful look. "As a matter of fact, it is," she said, putting the tray down on a table. "But don't get used to it. Mom was shocked when I told her you weren't out of bed two hours ago with the rest of the hands."

The smell of food coaxed Lisa from the comfort of her bed. Self-consciously she wrapped herself in her new blue bathrobe and hurried to the table. "Hot oatmeal and maple syrup. Mmmmmm."

"And homemade biscuits with gravy!" Carole cried with delight, joining her.

Kate slid into an armchair next to the potbellied stove. "Cowboys have biscuits with every meal," she said mournfully.

"Don't you like them?" Lisa asked around a mouthful of biscuit, butter, and gravy. The thought that her mother would have swooned at her bad manners somehow delighted her.

"They were great," Kate assured them. "Every day, for the first ten years of my life."

"Overkill," Carole laughed as she generously

covered her oatmeal with syrup. "Happens in everyone's family."

"Look, don't take too long eating," Kate said. "I have the whole day planned. It's a surprise. And you'll need an extra T-shirt."

"Does this 'something special' involve riding?" Lisa asked hopefully.

Kate rolled her eyes. "I can't believe you even need to ask. Get dressed and meet me at the corral. Only the paying customers get their horses saddled for them."

"I've got a couple of bucks," Carole offered between mouthfuls.

"That wouldn't even pay for valet parking these days," Kate said, lifting her nose in the air. "We do run a classy establishment, you know." She got halfway through the door and turned around. "Hey, Lisa, what did your mom pack for you this time?"

Lisa felt herself blush at the thought of all the fancy clothes her mother had insisted on buying her for the trip. She had tried to explain that all she needed were a few pairs of old jeans and a couple of shirts, but her mother refused to change her mind. "Don't worry, I buried my old stuff in the bottom of the suitcase while mom was out of the room."

Carole looked at her. "Taking a page out of Stevie's book?"

Lisa shrugged and grinned. "Learn from the best, that's my motto."

"Whatever," Kate told them. "Just get out here pronto, we're—"

"Burning daylight!" they finished for her.

Kate laughed. "I really have missed you guys." Then she disappeared out the door.

Urged on by the prospect of a day spent on horseback, Lisa and Carole gobbled their breakfast and threw on their oldest jeans, broken-in cowboy boots, and sweaters over light T-shirts, and they pulled their hair back in ponytails for maximum efficiency and minimum bother.

On their way to the corral, Lisa had a chance to observe some of the changes the ranch had undergone since their last visit. From the fresh paint on the barn to the new wood on the corrals, everything had an air of prosperity. "Looks like Kate's folks are doing okay," she observed.

"Glad to see it. They went through some close calls financially, remember?"

Lisa nodded. If anyone had deserved a break, it was the Devines. They were really nice, hardworking people.

"I hear they've had some personnel changes, though," Carole said tentatively.

Lisa noted her friend's hesitant look. "It's okay, I know he's not here anymore. You don't have to try to break it to me gently."

"Sorry. I wasn't sure if you'd heard. You and John . . ."

"John Brightstar was very special and he still is. I'm sure we'll see each other again," Lisa said firmly.

"Skye Ransom and John Brightstar . . . ," Carole muttered quietly.

Lisa frowned. "What about them?"

Carole broke into a wide grin. "You sure do have good taste."

That did it: Any clouds on Lisa's horizon were gone. She was at the Bar None with two of her best friends, on a sunny day with weeks left before school started. What more could she ask for?

Then she saw her. She was leaning against the rails of the corral, a gleam in her eyes and a bit in her mouth. Lisa's heart skipped a beat. "Chocolate," she whispered in wonder. "You beautiful creature!"

The Bay mare whinnied a greeting.

"Berry!" Carole called out delightedly to the strawberry roan beside her. "I knew you would wait for me."

The two girls scrambled through the fence and slipped their arms around the horses' necks.

"I take it you approve of the riding accommodations," a drawling voice said beside them.

Lisa disentangled herself from the horse. A young woman with a weathered cowboy hat pulled low over her eyes stepped out from the stable.

"Howdy, I'm Paula," she said, offering a leather-gloved hand.

Lisa shook it. By her estimation Paula was no more than five foot three and couldn't have weighed more than one hundred and five pounds even if her jeans, boots, and faded work shirt had been soaking wet.

"I'm Lisa. This is Carole."

"Nice to meet you," said Carole.

Kate joined them. "Oh good, you guys have met."

"Welcome to the Bar None," Paula said formally.

"Paula, these are my friends," Kate said.

Paula eyed them up and down. "The expert riders you told me about?"

Kate nodded. "Yep."

"Then why did I have to saddle their horses for them?"

Lisa felt embarrassed. "Jet lag?" she suggested apologetically.

43

Paula nodded mournfully. "Oh yeah, that's one of those city-folk diseases, isn't it? Makes you stay in bed all day for no good reason?"

Lisa felt herself blushing.

Carole stepped forward. "Sorry, Paula, won't happen again."

Paula smiled in a way that implied she was certain it would. "I have things to do, but I'm sure Kate won't mind showing you where the mounting block is." She trudged away.

"Mounting block?" Carole said indignantly.

"I know, I know," Kate said, throwing her hands up defensively. "She's kind of the Eeyore of the ranch, but she's actually very nice once you scratch the surface."

"We're only going to be here for a week," Lisa reminded her. "How deep do you think we'll get?"

"Paper cut, maybe. Flesh wound, tops."

All three girls burst into laughter.

"I can't wait to tell Stevie about her," Carole said. "Paula makes her cousin Dava look like Auntie Mame!"

Kate looked puzzled. "Who?"

"Auntie Mame," Carole reiterated. "From the old movie with Rosalind Russell."

"Lucille Ball played the part, too," Lisa offered help-fully. "In the musical version."

"True," Carole conceded, "but critics agree that Russell achieved the quintessential carefree, live-life-to-the-hilt spirit of the character to a much more satis-fying degree."

Nobody said anything for a moment.

"Of course, the musical version did have Robert Preston," Carole acknowledged.

Lisa and Kate remained mute.

Carole turned away and began fiddling with her horse's gear. "You know, we are burning daylight," she mumbled.

Kate and Lisa giggled.

"I have to stop by the house and grab our saddle-bags," Kate told them. "You two mount up and I'll meet you there."

Lisa hooked her left stirrup over the saddle horn and checked to make sure her horse's cinch was tight, then replaced her stirrup, gripped the saddle horn, and swung lightly up into place. She noticed someone had tied a small coil of rope to one side of the saddle. "Hey, Carole, what do you think this is for?"

Carole shrugged. "Beats me, but I have one, too. Do you think it has something to do with Kate's surprise?"

"She's taking us cow roping?"

"No, it's the wrong kind of rope for a lariat—that would be much stiffer. This stuff is soft cotton."

Lisa shrugged. "Well, the sooner we get started, the sooner we'll find out the answer." Gathering both reins in her left hand, she shifted her weight in preparation for a turn and was delighted to feel Chocolate already responding. She gave her an affectionate pat on the neck. "Atta girl."

When Carole was settled on Berry, the two of them set off at a lazy walk. They soon spied their friend, sitting astride her horse by the kitchen, with two bulging saddlebags secured to her saddle.

"Hey, Lisa, is that the horse I think it is?" Carole asked as they got nearer.

"It sure is," Lisa confirmed. "Stewball."

The pinto seemed to have recognized his name, because he turned his head in their direction.

"He looks great," Lisa told Kate, eyeing the animal affectionately.

"Oh, there's no keeping Stewball down." With no visible cueing, horse and rider swung in beside the other two. "We had him rounding up strays the last couple of weeks and he loved it, but we didn't want to

46

burn him out, so Dad said I could use him for pleasure riding this week."

"We'd better not mention this to Stevie," Carole cautioned. "You know how much she loves him."

Lisa nodded. "She used to say he was practically psychic."

"I'm not convinced she's wrong," Kate told them. "I've met a lot of horses with good cow sense over the years, but Stewball is something special."

"What's *cow sense?*" asked Lisa. She couldn't remember having heard the term before.

"A horse's ability to anticipate and outwit a cow. It's an invaluable trait in a working ranch horse. Some people say it's a taught skill, but all the old-timers I've ever talked to swear it's instinctive. The horse has to be born with it."

"And Stewball has that?"

"Stewball has that and a bit to spare. He's also got some mountain pony in him, so he's very surefooted."

"Remember how Stevie wanted to take him back East to work with her in dressage?" Carole reminisced. "She said with his ability to sense what his rider wants almost before his rider knows they want it, he could be a monster hit."

47

"But she was also smart enough to know that Stewball is where he belongs. He probably would have been a great show horse, but in his heart he loves working the ranch," Kate said. "He wouldn't have been as happy."

Lisa frowned. "Do you think we should tell her how content he is without her, or would that make her more miserable?"

"Actually, I think it would make her feel better," Carole told her.

Kate laughed. "Yeah, but you might want to rethink the wording a little bit."

They continued along, chatting easily about anything that came to mind.

The morning was faultless. The sky was a deep blue, and although the air was cool, Lisa knew it could easily be sweltering before noon. Looking back, she saw the trail the horses had left as they passed through the long dewy grass. Looking forward, she could see the beginning of a thick, lush forest. "Where are we going, anyway, Kate?"

"I told you, I have something wonderful to show you."

"How long will it take to get there?"

"As long as it takes."

"What a typical cowboy reply," Lisa grumbled good-naturedly.

"What's in the saddlebags?" Carole asked.

"Something special," Kate said, smiling.

"Aren't you going to tell us anything at all?"

"Yeah, have a little mercy," Lisa urged. "We're dying of curiosity here."

"You two will simply have to hold your horses."

"Tell me you didn't just say that!" cried Carole.

All the girls laughed.

"All right," Kate relented. "I'll say this much—you two are never going to forget this afternoon as long as you live!"

4

Dear Lisa, Carole, and Kate,
Got your e-mail.
Could you guys be having any more fun?
Sorry to hear that the airplane ride was a little turbulent, but you should have seen the air pockets my brothers let loose in the backseat of the van. Gross! Of course when I complained to Mom and Dad, what happened? They told me to stop whining! Okay, that wasn't the way they actually put it, but it was what they meant. I mean, they made it sound like all I had done the whole trip was complain. Gee, I can't think of what I might have to complain about, can you? I'm only being held hostage, in unspeakably crowded conditions, with basi-

cally inhuman companions, while being transported across state lines against my will, and when I get there I'll be tortured by the noxious droning of my stupid cousin Dava and deprived of the basic and simple right of physical exercise!!!

By the way, can either of you tell me the average size of a boy's bladder? Like a thimble maybe? Is it possible that miniature bladders are a genetic disorder that runs in my family? Luckily I seem to have been spared, but if the amount of times we had to make bathroom stops for my brothers is any indication, then the answer is a big yes! I mentioned my concern to my parents, explaining that I wasn't complaining but simply pointing out a medical crisis that I personally felt might be better addressed by our physician at home and my willingness to forgo the trip for the welfare of the many over the few. Pretty selfless of me, hmmm? I know, I know. They didn't buy it, either.

And, I swear, is counting cows not the stupidest game ever invented? That's right, counting cows! Whoever has the most cows on their side of the car at the end of the trip wins. That's pretty much the entire game. But you never heard such arguments over who had how many and who cheated in counting and who passed a cemetery (which means you lose all your

cows) and who cares! Torture, I tell you! Mile after
mile of sheer torture!

The worst moment came when I realized we had
passed over into Massachusetts and I was now not
only in the same country as Dava but in the same
state as well! HELP ME! I actually volunteered to let
my brothers bounce some more spitballs off the back
of my head in return for early parole back home.

Lesser people in my position would have given way
to despair by now, but I, Stevie Lake, am determined
to triumph over my tormentors. I will rise above,
and, failing that, I will take them all down in flames
with me! Ha ha ha ha!

Be sure to write me soon. I can't wait to hear more
about the great time you two are having.

Stevie paused with her finger hovering over the
Save button. Did that last bit sound insincere? She
quickly scanned the e-mail again, then added: *I've*
done my best to hide the true extent of my misery. After
all, I wouldn't want to ruin your vacation. It would obvi-
ously be too upsetting for the three of you to read how mis-
erable I really am. I'm holding back some of the gorier
details. Love, Stevie.

There was a knock on her hotel room door and her

mother poked her head in. "Stevie, are you about finished? It's almost time to go meet the Sinclairs for lunch."

"Awww, Mom, do I have—"

"Yes, you do," her mother replied firmly, cutting her off. Her eyes opened wide. "You're not even dressed!"

Stevie looked down at herself. She was wearing her favorite jeans, sneakers, and a comfortable shirt with the sleeves rolled up. "What do you mean?"

"Why aren't you wearing one of the new outfits I got you?"

Stevie cringed. Her mother had actually bought her a twin set—a short-sleeved sweater with a matching long-sleeved sweater to put over it. She'd look like the school librarian if she wore that. "I was saving them for an important occasion."

"Meeting your cousins for the first time in ages, in preparation for a wedding, is an important occasion," her mother informed her through gritted teeth.

Stevie looked sullenly at the floor.

"Please, honey," her mother coaxed. "You know Dava will give you a hard time if you show up like that. You don't want to give her any ammo, do you?"

That hit home. Stevie was definitely reluctant to let Dava hold anything over her. In fact, the more she considered it, this luncheon might be the perfect opportunity to set her cousin straight on some of the uglier facts of life. Maybe she could even sic her twin brother, Alex, on the girl.

"Do it for your father and me, won't you?"

Stevie began to peel off her clothes. "Okay, Mom. I wouldn't want to let our side of the family down." She grinned wickedly into the inside of her tank-top. *After all, I have a reputation to maintain.*

CAROLE FOLLOWED KATE through the dense forest, her horse picking his way easily along the narrow trail. The air was scented with the smell of pine, and the rhythmic sound of Berry's hooves striking the ground was almost hypnotic. A mile or so back they had left the flatlands and were now going up a steep incline. Every once in a while the trees and shrubbery would thin enough for the girls to catch a breathtaking view of the surrounding mountains and valley below. Carole sighed happily. "You are so lucky," she told Kate. "Look where you get to live."

"Look how she gets to ride," Lisa said. "I almost feel like I'm cheating when I ride Western."

Carole nodded. "Me too. This big old saddle is kind of like an easy chair, and since we get to keep our

54

stirrups longer than in an English saddle, there isn't as much strain on the legs and back."

"That was exactly the idea when they developed Western riding," Kate explained. "The pioneers had to travel long distances on horseback, so they made it as comfortable and practical as possible."

Carole was watching Stewball ambling along in front of her. "The horses even seem to move differently from those back home."

"A trail horse's paces were developed for maximum comfort. Their gaits are smooth and flat, so the horse uses a lot less knee and hock action. Most other kinds of riding encourage horses to put spring and tension in their paces. It looks prettier, but it's harder on the animal's legs and joints."

"Not to mention the rider's butt," cracked Lisa.

Carole resisted the urge to collect her horse—to remind Berry who was in charge and to perk up his ambling gait. She understood that the way to ride a Western horse was to keep contact with its mouth to a minimum, but after all her years of English training, it made her feel like she was letting her horse be sloppy.

"A good trail horse needs to be calm and relaxed, easy to handle," Kate said.

Carole noted Stewball's flopping ears. "If Stewball

gets much more relaxed, we're going to have to call him a cab."

"Appearances can be deceiving," Kate answered. In a flash her horse had spun 180 degrees to face Lisa and Carole with pricked ears and wide-open eyes. Kate smiled at the other girls' astonished expressions. "Out here we call that a rollback." Once again Stewball whipped into action, this time making a full 360-degree turn, spinning on his hindquarters. "And that," she said, sweeping her cowboy hat off and bowing, "was a pirouette."

Lisa's mouth hung open with admiration. "Wow, that was great! I hardly saw you doing anything. It was like Stewball did it all on his own."

"He almost did. He's been doing those moves so long, all I had to do was give him a hint of what I wanted."

Carole was also impressed. "And I thought he was about to nod off."

"Oh, he was just conserving his energy. A seasoned trail horse will do that so that he has it to use when he really needs it."

They were standing on the edge of a meadow carpeted with wildflowers. A sea of snowy white, sunshine yellow, and lipstick red blossoms quivered in the breeze, attended and nurtured by an army of flitting butterflies, bees, and dragonflies.

Kate eyed the meadow speculatively. "What do you say to using up some of the horses' batteries?"

Carole felt her heart twitch with excitement. "Gallop?"

"This meadow is nice and level, but let me and Stewball lead the way, okay?"

Lisa and Carole were only too happy to agree.

"Yee haw!" Kate shouted, urging Stewball into action.

"Yee haw!" Carole and Lisa cried, following.

In a flash they were tearing across the meadow.

Carole felt her horse's powerful hindquarters gathering and releasing, sending the two of them charging forward. She leaned down closer to Berry's bobbing neck, going with his motion and urging him on. The wind whipped up his mane, and it lashed her cheeks. She relished the feeling.

All too soon they reached the end of the open area and pulled reluctantly to a halt. The horses snorted and nodded their heads, eyes bright and tails twitching.

Carole laughed with unabashed delight. "Yesss!"

"It doesn't get any better than this," Lisa declared.

"Wait until you see what's coming," Kate said mysteriously.

"What could possibly beat galloping a wonderful horse across an amazing field of wildflowers on a gorgeous day with two of your very best friends in the world?" Lisa asked.

Kate leaned forward. "Show 'em for me, will you, Stewball?"

With a gentle snort her horse headed off at an eager walk.

"He knows where we're going?" Carole asked skeptically.

"Of course. I told him this morning," Kate replied lightly.

Lisa's eyes met Carole's. "That's some horse."

Kate called back over her shoulder. "Come on, we're almost there."

As they rode on, Lisa and Carole continued to admire the passing landscape, oohing and ahhing over the exceptional scenery. After a short time Kate disappeared from view over the top of a small rise. When Carole crested the hill, she pulled Berry to a halt, hardly able to believe her eyes.

Below her, the woods fell away to reveal one of the most beautiful sights she had ever seen—a pond of the deepest, purest blue fed by a roaring waterfall, which spilled down a sheer rock cliff. The water sparkled in the early afternoon sunshine, and its edges reflected the surrounding meadow. The grass was so lush it looked like someone had colored it all with a single shade of green paint. Magnificent trees, whose leaves rustled in the soft breeze, invited them to shelter in their shade from the growing heat of the day. One tree arched its branches far out over the water, and some enterprising person had tied a long, thick rope to one of them.

"It's spectacular," Lisa murmured.

Carole thought that was an understatement. "*National Geographic* should see this."

Kate was already off her horse and waving at them from below. "Come on," she urged. "It's all ours."

The girls didn't need to be told twice. They eased their horses down the gentle slope to the waiting paradise below, joining Kate under one of the choicest trees.

"Last one in is a rotten egg," Kate yelled, pulling off her boots.

"But Kate, we can't go swimming," Lisa lamented. "We didn't bring our bathing suits."

"You've got T-shirts and undies, don't you?"

"Yes."

Kate pulled off her jeans. "That's more than they had in Eden."

Carole almost laughed out aloud at the shocked look on Lisa's face. "Come on, Lisa, there's no one here but us," she said, following Kate's lead. "And I'm not sure this isn't Eden."

"I did it the other day when I found this place. I don't think anyone else on the planet knows about it."

"I guess it's not like we'd be skinny-dipping," Lisa said cautiously.

Carole was struggling out of her own clothes. "That's the spirit."

Lisa threw herself on the ground and began yanking at her boots with enthusiasm. "We'better take care of the horses first, though. I bet they're thirsty."

"Can we give them a drink from the pond?" Carole asked Kate, who was unsaddling Stewball.

"The water's great for drinking—rocky mountain pure—but I have something else in mind for the horses. Get their stuff off and give me those ropes I put on your saddles."

Carole hurried to obey. *What is she up to?*

Moving quickly, Kate made the soft ropes into makeshift hackamores—bitless bridles. Carole admired her technique and made a mental note to ask her to teach them how to do it.

Kate surveyed her work. "All right, everybody on board. Any of you tenderfoots need a leg up?"

"We're going bareback riding in our underwear?" Lisa said doubtfully.

Carole understood her concern. Bareback riding in a bathing suit might look glamorous in a television commercial, but in reality it would cause a nasty rash on the inside of your thighs from rubbing against the horse's hair.

"Nope. We're going swimming and the horses are going to join us," Kate announced triumphantly, mounting Stewball with ease.

Carole scrambled up on Berry, thankful that he wasn't as big a horse as her own, Starlight, was. "Are you sure about this?"

Kate led the way to the edge of the water. "They love it," she assured them. "Horses are natural swimmers. Cowboys use them to cross raging rivers they're unable to swim themselves."

If Carole had any doubts, they were quickly banished when Berry headed for the water with obvious eagerness. Moments later she found herself sitting with her feet submerged while her horse satisfied his thirst.

Stewball, having already quenched his, was pawing playfully at the mirrorlike surface. He blew noisily when he accidentally splashed some water up his nose.

"Carole," Lisa cried, "look at me!"

She turned to see her usually cautious friend up to her waist in water and Chocolate's head bobbing up and down as she swam in an easy circle.

Not wanting to be left out, Carole encouraged Berry to go deeper. The water rose around her, and she felt Berry swimming eagerly forward. She reveled in this unique experience and felt a wide smile stretching across her face.

After a while, Kate called them out. "I think the horses have had enough for now. We can tie them to the trees and let them graze while they dry off."

As soon as the horses were secured, the girls headed back into the water.

It turned out that Kate was the one who had tied the rope to the branch stretching over the water. The girls took turns swinging on it and seeing who could jump the farthest. With no grown-ups to tell them to be quiet, they all felt free to do exactly as they wished, which meant whooping and hollering and splashing like maniacs. Finally they crept onto a dry boulder to warm up in the sunshine.

Lisa climbed to her feet. "I claim this land in the name of The Saddle Club," she declared to the world.

Kate and Carole dissolved into giggles.

Carole shivered happily, stretching her T-shirt down over her knees and hugging them. She couldn't remember feeling happier in her whole life. "I don't know about you two, but I'm ravenous."

Kate jumped from the boulder to the shore. "Say no more. Mom packed us a huge lunch. Fried chicken, cheese, pickles, fresh apple pie, and . . ."

"Homemade biscuits?" Carole guessed.

Kate nodded. "What else? Come on, let's chow down."

The girls ate a sumptuous meal sitting in the grass under the trees. They washed everything down with fresh water from the waterfall, which Kate caught in her canteen.

Everyone agreed it was the finest day ever.

All too soon it was time to get dressed and head back.

"It's a longer ride than you think," Kate warned them as she packed up.

"Oh no!" Lisa cried, jumping to her feet from where she had sat to pull on her boots.

"It's not that bad," Carole assured her.

"It's not the ride home," Lisa said mournfully. "It's the e-mail."

They all shuddered at the thought. How were they ever going to make this day sound dull to Stevie?

IT WAS UNBELIEVABLE. *I almost fell over when she said it. "I love horses, I've been such a fool."* Those were Dava's exact words!

It was after supper at the Bar None, and Carole, Lisa, and Kate were gathered around the computer, unable to believe what they were reading in Stevie's latest e-mail.

I was all prepared for a miserable afternoon and it turned out okay. In fact, better than okay. We talked about horses almost the whole time. It turns out that Dava and some friends went on a pleasure ride at a local stable. Actually, she confessed she only went along because a boy she liked was going. Anyway,

65

she ended up loving it. She kept talking about how wonderful Boddington is. That's the name of the horse she rode. She doesn't know a lot about horses yet, but she said she's eager to learn. She wants to take lessons, and she asked me to help talk her folks into it. Of course I said I'd be happy to.

I swear it's almost like she had a personality transplant, and none too soon.

Anyway, I wanted you guys to know that things are looking up here. I really think everything's going to turn out all right after all.

Write soon.

Love, Stevie

"This is so great!" Carole exclaimed.

Lisa, who was sitting at the keyboard, couldn't have agreed more. "You know what this means, don't you? It means we can tell her the truth about today."

"You go first with the picnic, and then I'll fill her in on the truth about the plane ride," Carole suggested eagerly.

It took them a long time to finish the message to their mutual satisfaction. Finally they sent it off into cyberspace, and they all fell into bed, exhausted and satisfied.

The next day, Lisa and Carole rose bright and early, determined to show everybody they could pull their own weight around the ranch. They made it to the ranch house in time for breakfast with the rest of the hands. Lisa couldn't help noticing Paula's look of surprise when they walked in.

"So, you two ready for another hard day of picnicking?" she chuckled, clearing her plate from the table.

Lisa looked over at Kate. "Actually, I don't know what we're doing today," she confessed.

"Come on, Paula, give them a break," Kate coaxed. "Yesterday was their first day here. They deserved a treat."

Paula shrugged as if it was a matter of pure indifference to her. "Whatever, but some of us have real work to do."

"Anything we could help with?" Lisa offered.

"Doubt it," Paula replied brusquely. Wiping her hands on her jeans, she strode out the door.

The girls took their places at the table next to Kate.

"I don't get it. What did we do to make her dislike us so much?" Carole asked, buttering a thick slab of toast.

Kate shook her head. "I don't know. I only told her good things about you."

"Like what?"

"Well . . . like how Stevie could make any horse dance on the head of a pin."

Carole nodded. "But what did you tell her about Lisa and me?"

Kate considered a moment while she nibbled unenthusiastically on a piece of crisp bacon. "I told her that you can jump a horse through the eye of a needle without brushing the edges, and that Lisa is a riding prodigy who learns so fast she would probably be able to do Paula's job almost as well as she could by the end of the visit."

Lisa groaned. "No wonder she doesn't like us. She must think we have heads bigger than this entire state."

"You think I overdid it then?" Kate said sheepishly.

Carole patted her on the back. "Yeah, but thanks for the compliments."

"I think we should show her we're not really so bad," Lisa said thoughtfully. "I hate to leave her with such a negative opinion of us."

"What can we do?" Carole asked. "What does Paula admire in people, Kate?"

Kate smiled. "Hard work."

After a hasty breakfast the day passed in a whirl of activity. Buoyed by a determination to prove themselves

68

worthy to the touchy wrangler, the girls tackled chore after chore: moving a small herd of cattle from one paddock to another, cleaning tack, getting horses ready for the guests, feeding the animals, shoveling manure. They did anything and everything that was asked of them. They even helped prepare and serve the dinner for the staff and guests that evening.

Lisa wiped her hands on a kitchen towel and collapsed in a chair. "That's it. Every last pot is scrubbed and every last dish is dried."

"You girls certainly deserve time off for good behavior," Kate's mother told them. "I want you to have some fun tomorrow." With that, she shooed them out of the kitchen.

"You know, it actually was a fun day," Carole said as she booted up the computer to e-mail Stevie.

Lisa frowned. "The only bad part is, as hard as we worked, I didn't see Paula all day. Which means she didn't see us, either."

"Guess you'll have to be satisfied with a job well done," Kate told her.

"I can live with that."

"Oh no, I don't believe it," Carole groaned, staring at the computer screen. "You guys had better have a look at this."

They gathered around her to read Stevie's latest e-mail.

What a double-dealing two-faced cat that Dava has turned out to be! It was all an act! She totally suckered me in! She never loved horses, except for a stuffed one a friend gave her. She said she couldn't resist teasing me. I can't stand her—I'd like to wipe that self-satisfied little smirk off her face. What a cow! I would rather spend an entire afternoon with Veronica diAngelo than one more minute with Dava! Yes, she's actually that bad. But I can't get away from her. This afternoon I have to go to Robin's bridal shower, and Dava's going to be there, too.

You guys, on the other hand, seem to be having the time of your lives. That picnic sounded like pure heaven, and right now I'd give my right arm to take Stewball for a ride. Actually I'd give Dava's right arm to go for a ride on any horse. In fact, I'd give both of Dava's arms, plus her legs, her scrawny stick-thin body, and her head. Especially her head! I've never been more miserable.

But don't worry about me. Keep having a great time. I'll be fine. Really.

Missing you, Stevie

"She sounds really desperate," Kate said.

Carole nodded. "Yeah. That line about Veronica is a dead giveaway."

"That's her mortal enemy back at your riding stable, right?" Kate asked.

"Uh-huh. Stevie volunteering to spend time with her is like Dorothy offering to hang with the Wicked Witch of the West," Lisa told her. "I wish there was something we could do to help."

Carole gave a hearty sigh. "At least our e-mail back won't be overly exciting. I'll tell her about how Paula doesn't like us."

"Yeah," said Lisa. "And don't forget to mention all the chores Kate made us do."

"I did not!"

"Be sure to describe the agony of my dishpan hands after she insisted we wash all the dishes," Lisa continued.

"I did not," Kate repeated. "You guys volunteered!" She put her hands on her hips. "If you're so exhausted, maybe you shouldn't come with me tomorrow."

Lisa was filled with anticipation. "Where? Is it as good as the pond?"

Kate shrugged. "Different."

Lisa and Carole tried to press her for more details,

71

but it was no use. They were going to have to wait to find out about Kate's next surprise.

LISA WAS THE first out of bed. She roused Carole, who yawned and stretched and scratched at her ankle. "The local fauna picking on you?" Lisa asked sympathetically as she slipped into her old jeans, feeling a twinge of guilt that she hadn't actually worn any of the new clothes her mother had bought her yet.

"Guess so. If there's a mosquito within a mile, I'm the one it heads for," Carole lamented. "Hey, Kate! Up and at 'em!"

Kate slowly sat up in bed and, with hardly a word, began to pull on her clothes.

Lisa was surprised. Usually Kate bounded out of bed full of life and fun. "Everything okay?" she asked tentatively.

"I didn't sleep well, that's all. I couldn't seem to get comfortable."

"You still want to go out today?" Carole asked.

"Let me see. I can stay at the ranch and do more chores, or I can take my friends on another adventure." She gave Carole a smile. "You do the math."

"We're outta here!" Carole and Lisa exclaimed.

The day's plans were almost derailed by Mrs. Devine

at breakfast. "Kate," she said with concern, "You look a little flushed. Are you all right?"

Kate dodged the hand her mother put out to feel her forehead. "I'm fine, Mom."

"Well, okay," her mother said. "Maybe some fresh air would do you good."

The girls saddled up and headed off, this time with Kate taking them in the opposite direction of the pond. After a brief ride over a few hills and through a small wooded area, Kate announced they were there.

The girls sat on their horses and looked over a deep horseshoe-shaped canyon. From their position at the rounded curve of the back of the horseshoe, Lisa could see the rocky left and right branches stretching away on either side of them. The steep walls looked treacherous and uninviting. "Exactly what are we doing here?" She gulped, backing chocolate a little farther from the edge.

Kate pulled her neckerchief off and wiped at her sweaty forehead. "Prepare to journey with me back through time," she announced grandly. "Back to the days when dinosaurs ruled the earth!"

Carole guffawed. "Have you been out in the sun too long?"

Lisa did think Kate looked overheated.

Kate urged Stewball down a rocky slope. "Forward, nonbelievers!"

Moving cautiously, the horses sent tiny rivers of rocks rolling down the steep grade before them. Lisa was glad Chocolate was such a reliable horse; a fall down these rocks would be a nasty experience.

At the bottom, Kate paused in front of a house-sized boulder. "The doorway to the past is the doorway to the future."

"Will you stop already?" Carole told her. "Pretty soon you'll be gazing into crystal balls and reading tea leaves."

Kate laughed. "All right, come on. I want to introduce you to some friends." She led them around the boulder and into a beehive of activity.

Lisa pulled Chocolate to a halt, staring with wonder at the sight in front of her.

Much of the floor of the canyon had been roped off into small sections. There were people everywhere. Some were pushing what appeared to be wheelbarrows full of dirt from place to place; others were meticulously sifting the soil through large screens. A few individuals were simply crouching in place, staring fixedly at the ground. Lisa could even see distant figures standing on a scaffold suspended high up on the canyon wall.

"What on earth is going on here?" Lisa asked. "Are they building something?"

"This looks like an archaeological dig," Carole said almost breathlessly.

Kate clucked Stewball forward. "That's exactly what it is. Can you believe our luck? The university has started a dinosaur dig practically in the Bar None's backyard!"

Lisa was enthralled. She had always wanted to see a real dig in action. In her fantasies it had always been somewhere in Egypt, with pyramids and mummies scattered around, but dinosaurs were even better. "When did they get here?"

"At the beginning of summer. I was going to tell you over the phone, but then I decided to make it a surprise. Come on, I'll introduce you to Professor Jackson. He's the paleontologist in charge of the whole thing."

"He won't mind our being here?" Lisa asked.

"Naw, I've been down here lots of times. He said I could come by whenever I want. I think he's hoping to recruit me as another worker," she laughed.

"What a great opportunity," Lisa said enthusiastically, hurrying to catch up.

Kate led the way toward a small group of tents nestled against the valley wall. As the girls moved through the dig, she called and waved to several of the workers, who smiled and waved back. "There he is," she said, pointing to a short, skinny man bending over a folding table. His clothes were dusty and rumpled, and he was mopping his face with a faded red handkerchief. He removed his hat, revealing a nearly bald head with unruly tufts of white fluff.

"Doesn't look much like Indiana Jones, does he?" Carole giggled.

"He's the real thing," Kate told her seriously. "Professor Jackson is very distinguished in his field. A private museum is paying a lot of money to have him head this dig for them."

Lisa considered that. "I didn't realize there was a lot of money to be made in archaeology."

The girls dismounted and Kate led them up to the table. "Hi, Professor. I brought my friends to meet you."

Professor Jackson looked up. "Ah, Kate, my dear. Welcome." He swept a pair of wire-rimmed glasses off his nose and perched them jauntily on his head. "Brought me a few diggers, have you?"

Kate nodded. "That's me, Slaves-R-Us. Their folks will never miss them, but make sure the money is in my bank account by sundown."

Professor Jackson clucked his tongue. "First we'll have to see how good they are."

"This is Lisa and Carole," said Kate, making the introductions. "They're from Willow Creek, near Washington, D.C."

"Is that so? I'm afraid I haven't had the pleasure of working in your part of the country."

"We only have a rock quarry," Lisa said, then felt herself redden. *What a goofy thing to say.*

The professor smiled at her. "Some interesting things have turned up in rock quarries, my dear. But this part of the country does seem to have more than its fair share of artifacts. Who knows? This canyon may prove to be as famous as Dinosaur National Monument when we're finished."

"Dinosaur what?" Carole asked.

The professor looked surprised. "You've never heard of it?"

Lisa and Carole shook their heads.

"It's an area covering about three hundred and thirty square miles in northwest Colorado and Utah. It's protected by the government because of all the rich fossil remains they've found there," Kate told them, looking superior. "They've even found dinosaurs, which is how it got its name."

77

"I see you've been doing your homework since we last spoke," the professor said.

"Let me guess," Lisa whispered in Kate's ear. "You looked that up last night."

Her friend blushed.

"By the way, have you been introduced to Joanne?" the professor asked.

Lisa shook her head.

"Then we shall have to fix that right away."

"We wouldn't want to interrupt your work, professor," Carole said politely.

Lisa was disappointed. She was dying to find out more, and who better than the professor to teach them?

"It so happens I'm heading in that direction," he said, looking at his watch. "It's time for me to check in with the guards anyway."

"Guards?" Lisa asked. "Why would you need guards?"

"Just because these bones have been hanging around for between 65 and 245 million years doesn't mean there aren't a lot of people competing to dig them up," he told her. "A dinosaur skeleton in reasonable condition would bring a large amount of money on the black market."

Lisa was amazed. "There's a black market for dinosaur bones?"

"Unfortunately, yes." He stopped next to a roped-off section of ground. "There are a lot of wealthy people in this world who like to collect unique treasures such as these and keep them locked away for only themselves to view." He shook his head sadly. "And there are a lot of unscrupulous people who will stop at nothing to provide them with those items, as long as the price is right."

"Wow. I had no idea it was such a cutthroat business," Carole said, wide-eyed.

The professor laughed. "I'm afraid I'm prone to exaggeration, as some of my students will be happy to tell you. Usually digging through miles of dirt under the hot sun is as about as adventurous as it gets."

"But sometimes you do find whole dinosaur skeletons, don't you?" Kate prodded.

"They are few and very far between," said a young woman who was coming to the professor's side. "But Professor Jackson has dug up more than his fair share." She swatted him lightly on the shoulder with obvious affection. "How am I going to make my reputation if you won't leave anything for the rest of us to discover?"

"Just the person I was looking for," Professor Jackson said with a smile. "Girls, allow me to introduce you to Joanne, my greatest student."

Joanne was of medium height with dark curly hair pulled back in a low ponytail. Her worn pants and old work boots were caked with dust, and her arms and face were deeply tanned. She nodded at the girls in a friendly but preoccupied way, then held out a small notebook. "More like your greatest disappointment today, I'm afraid."

The professor took the book and scanned the pages. "No luck in the fourth quadrant?" he asked with a frown.

"Not yet," she replied.

Lisa noticed that Kate was cricking her neck like it was bothering her. *Maybe she's bored,* she thought with surprise. Lisa, on the other hand, was absolutely fascinated. She wanted very much to learn more about all this, and the best way to do that, she always found, was to get some hands-on experience. "Is there anything we could help with?" she ventured, throwing caution to the wind. "I know we don't have any training, but we'd be happy to do anything." She saw Carole and Kate giving her astonished looks, but she ignored them. "We're really good with wheelbarrows," she added, avoiding her friends' eyes.

Professor Jackson looked pleased. "I don't know

about wheelbarrow duty," he said thoughtfully. "We try to get most of that out of the way in the mornings and evenings. Too hot in the afternoons."

Lisa could sense Carole's and Kate's relief, but she was determined to make herself useful. "Isn't there anything?"

"What do you say, Joanne? Can you use a few more sifters?"

"Are you kidding? I never turn down a free set of hands."

"I'll leave you to it, then," the professor replied. "See you later, girls."

True to her word, Joanne showed the three of them how to sift huge amounts of dirt through finer and finer mesh boxes. At first the girls were all enthralled, waiting for the sand to reveal some long-buried treasure, but as the day wore on and nothing significant surfaced, Lisa noticed Carole looking bored and Kate pausing to stretch her back more and more often. Finally Joanne reappeared.

"Sorry, guys, I got caught up in something." She observed the size of the pile of dirt they had sifted and seemed impressed.

"I don't know if we found anything important, but I

saved everything that looked even slightly unusual," Lisa informed her, pointing to a box.

"I told her they were only rocks and pebbles, but she insisted," Carole grumbled.

Lisa gave Carole a withering look and eagerly accompanied Joanne over to the box. To her disappointment, Carole turned out to be right. There were no dinosaur bones to be found, not even a lizard tooth.

Nevertheless, Joanne seemed very pleased with her attention to detail. "You know, Lisa, you may have the kind of patience it takes to be a good archaeologist."

Lisa beamed. "I've never really considered it as a career before."

Joanne looked at the other girls, who appeared to be quickly wilting in the heat of the day. "Why don't you two take a break," she suggested. "We have some cold refreshments in one of the tents."

Carole and Kate nodded gratefully.

"Lisa, would you like to help me with something else? It takes patience, but personally it's one of my favorite things to do on a dig."

Lisa was flattered to be asked. "I'd love to."

"Okay. Get yourself a quick drink and meet me at section eighty-five." Joanne pointed to a particular lot staked out with ropes.

The refreshment tent wasn't hard to find. The outside consisted of a raised awning that sheltered a few folding tables and chairs. Inside there were chests of iced sodas and large containers of fresh water. The girls helped themselves, then collapsed at a table in the shade.

"You don't look so good, Kate," Carole said.

Kate mopped at her face with her neckerchief. "I'm fine, but after sweating in the sun, this wind is giving me the shivers," she said irritably.

Lisa wasn't sure what to make of that. She was grateful for the slightest breeze. She finished her water and stood up. "I have to go help Joanne. I'll find you in a little while."

The two girls waved her off, and she made her way back to where Joanne was waiting.

"Good for you, Lisa. I like promptness in a person. Now look what we've got here. . . ."

Lisa knelt down and her eyes went wide. A genuine skeleton! "What is it?"

"An ancient species of bird."

"How do you know it's not one that died here a year ago?"

"The depth at which it was found gives us an idea of how long it's been here. The deeper down in the dirt, the older it is. In theory, at least," Joanne told her.

"See the delicate bones of the wing? We need to expose the rest of them."

"Wow!" Lisa said excitedly. "How do we get it out of the dirt?"

"We don't. We want to remove the dirt from it and leave the body just the way we found it until it can be photographed."

"Why?"

Joanne smiled at her. "You have an inquiring mind, Lisa. That's a real gift. The answer is that the position of the body can give us clues as to how it died."

Lisa shook her head. "What do you mean, how it died?"

"For instance, did it break its neck or did it simply die of natural causes? Maybe something killed it and ate it, and if that's the case, we might be able to figure out what the predator was by any tooth marks it may have left on the bones. That would help us deduce what other species existed here at the same time as this bird."

"Wow!" Lisa said again. "This is really interesting."

"I think so, too," Joanne said. "Now, here's what we're going to do." From a piece of rolled-up leather she extracted a paintbrush. "Very slowly, one grain at a time if necessary, you and I are going to finish unearthing this creature."

84

Lisa spent the remainder of her time at the dig working with the paintbrushes. Joanne demonstrated how a deft touch was needed to move minute pieces of dirt from a tiny area and scan it for possible significant remnants. Lisa found herself absolutely fascinated by the possibilities of what each stroke might reveal, and the time flew by. When Carole and Kate eventually showed up, it came as a shock to learn she had been at it for well over an hour.

"Do you mind if we head home now, Lisa?" Kate asked. "I'm not feeling very good."

Lisa was a little alarmed by her friend's flushed face and feverish-looking eyes. "You don't look so good, either. We'd better get you home."

Kate nodded wearily and led the way back to the horses.

During the ride home, Carole talked about a tent they had discovered that was full of unearthed treasures from the site. "You should have seen it, Lisa. They had all kinds of bones and stuff."

Lisa nodded absently. She was keeping a sharp eye on Kate, who seemed to be growing steadily worse.

"Professor Jackson said they were getting ready to send a shipment back to the museum for safekeeping," Carole continued. "I guess they do that when they think they have too many valuable things lying around. Did you know horses were the size of pigs a long time ago?"

"There's the ranch," Lisa said, a wave of relief washing over her. "We're almost there, Kate."

Kate turned and nodded weakly, then her eyes rolled back and she collapsed in her saddle.

As KATE SLID forward onto Stewball's neck, the horse came to a complete stop. He stood absolutely still, as though he knew that the slightest movement would dislodge his rider.

Quickly Lisa and Carole dismounted and hurried over to their stricken friend, only to find her eyes closed and her face flushed and sweating.

Carole shook her gently. "Kate?"

Slowly the girl opened her eyes. They were bright with fever. "Carole?" she mumbled with surprise, struggling upright in the saddle. "What happened?"

"I think you passed out," Lisa told her.

"It's so cold," she complained, shivering.

"Cold? It's like a hundred degrees out here," Lisa whispered to Carole.

"Should I go for help?" Carole asked.

Lisa scanned the distance to the ranch house. "We're almost there. Do you think you can make it if Carole and I ride on either side of you?"

Kate nodded wearily.

The girls quickly remounted and moved into position.

Kate leaned forward, and for one alarming moment Lisa thought she was going to pass out again, but she simply murmured in Stewball's ear. "Let's go home, boy."

Without further urging, the horse headed straight as an arrow for the Bar None. When he reached the corral, where most horses would have automatically stopped, he kept going, refusing to be sidetracked until he had reached the main house.

Carole jumped off Berry and rushed to help Kate down. Lisa bolted inside to get Mrs. Devine.

Kate's mother immediately took over, helping her daughter first into a cool shower and then into bed with a good dose of fever medicine.

"Don't worry, Mom," Kate protested. "I got too much sun, that's all."

"Looks more like the flu to me," her mother told

her, placing a pitcher of water on the bedside table within easy reach.

"But it's not flu season, Mom."

"Sleep is the best thing for you," Mrs. Devine told her firmly. "Call if you need anything, honey." She kissed her daughter on the forehead and guided Lisa and Carole out of the room.

"I don't like that fever," she said, turning to them in the hallway. "If she's not better by morning, I'm going to call the doctor."

"Is there anything we can do to help?" Carole asked.

"No. You two got her home safe, and that's enough for now. Why don't you relax?"

"Would you mind if we used the computer? We'd like to e-mail Stevie."

"That would be fine, girls," Mrs. Devine said absently. "I'll call you for dinner."

When the girls signed on, they were surprised to find nothing from their friend in Massachusetts.

"What do you think, Lisa? A good sign or bad?"

Lisa considered for a moment. "Good, I guess. Maybe she finally found something more interesting to do than write us with all her complaints."

Carole held up crossed fingers. "We can only hope. Now, what should we tell her about today?"

"Obviously we have to downplay the dinosaur dig."

"Gee," Carole said sarcastically. "Sifting dirt in the blazing sun for hours and hours and finding absolutely nothing . . . how could we possibly downplay that?"

"I enjoyed it."

Carole shrugged. "Whatever. I know, we can tell her how Kate has the flu and that her mom may not let her out riding for the rest of the visit."

"Wait a minute. Mrs. Devine didn't say that," Lisa protested.

"She didn't *not* say it, either," Carole pointed out. "Besides, we have to be creative here. We're suppose to be having a terrible time, remember?"

"Oh, yeah."

"Here," said Carole, pushing Lisa away from the keyboard and taking her place. "Let me do it."

Lisa watched, intrigued, as Carole carefully crafted a tale of endless work, thankless chores, and raging pestilence.

"You know, Carole, you're getting really good at this," she said, reading over her friend's shoulder.

Carole put her arms behind her head and leaned back with a satisfied smile. "I know. This one is practically a work of art."

———

THURSDAY EVENING, TWO days before the wedding and one day before the big rehearsal dinner, the Lake family pulled up outside the Sinclairs' house for yet another gathering of the immediate family.

Stevie stared at the house through the van window. It was a white two-story place with a spacious front lawn that was somewhat overwhelmed by a couple of giant spruce trees. A winding path bordered by cheerful flowers led the way up to the front door. All the windows were brightly lit, and party music filtered out into the sultry summer twilight.

Stevie leaned close to her window and fogged it with her breath, making the house disappear. *If only it were that easy*, she thought.

"The main party is going to be inside," Mrs. Lake informed them. "But Margaret said she would put some things outside for you kids as well."

"Oh, good, mosquito central," Stevie muttered, drawing a frowning face in the vapor on the glass. Although she had slathered herself with insect repellent, she doubted very much that it would do any good. "Can I wait here in the air-conditioned, mosquito-free van?"

"The porch area is screened in," her mother reminded her.

"Great. Trapped like a rat in a cage."

"If you get restless, you're welcome to run free. The Sinclairs own several acres of land behind the house. It almost makes me want to move here."

Stevie shuddered at the very thought.

"Stevie, get out," Alex said, shoving her. "You're holding everyone up."

"You should be thanking me," she told him as she reluctantly slid open the door. "The mosquitoes aren't the only bloodsuckers around here."

"Why are you always moaning about Dava, anyway?" he asked, scrambling out behind her. "She's not so bad."

"For a girl," her younger brother, Michael, said.

Stevie watched as Alex adjusted his baggy pants and fastened the top button of his shirt.

"How can you wear it like that?" she asked. "It's ninety degrees out here, with ninety percent humidity."

"Yeah," he acknowledged. "But the babes dig it."

"You mean Dava and her friends?" she said in her most scathing tone of voice. "Babes? I can't believe you don't see right through her."

"She's cute, and she has some cool CDs. What can I say? She's okay by me."

"But she's so mean!" Stevie raged.

"That's enough, Stevie," her father warned. "We're

all going inside now, and I want you on your best behavior. End of discussion."

Stevie shuffled down the path to the door behind the rest of her family. "Dead man walking!" she cried.

Her dad shot her a stern look. "Knock it off."

Stevie sighed. The door opened and her family was greeted warmly. Everyone but her, it seemed.

That suits me just fine, she thought, sliding along a wall to avoid the crush of people. *I'll get myself a plate of nibblies and a soda and find a corner of the room to hole up in. With any luck I won't have to speak to anyone the whole night.*

Careful to avoid all eye contact, Stevie made her way to the hors d'oeuvres table, piled a plate with goodies, and headed for the back door. She almost made it.

"Why, Steeevie, how nice to see you," Dava crooned from where she stood amid a small group of boys and girls. "And there's so much of you to see." Her eyes landed on the plate of food. "Oh, how thoughtful of you to bring enough for everyone. Ooops, I'm sorry, that's just for you, isn't it?" Dava's friends laughed.

Stevie could have died from humiliation, even though she knew very well she wasn't even close to being fat. "Dava, why don't you go . . . eat a cookie," she replied through gritted teeth.

"Why don't you eat one for me?" Dava said tartly.

"In that outfit, it looks like she ate one for all of us," one of the other girls snickered.

Stevie glared. Taking the potential mosquito problem into consideration, and having a general dislike for dressing up, she had chosen to wear deep purple cotton slacks that flared at the ankle and a very loose gauzy white top that she had hoped would work like mosquito netting. Her long hair was pulled back with a headband that matched the color of her pants, and she had selected black ankle boots with chunky heels to finish the outfit. Now she noticed with dismay that the other girls at the party were all wearing flirty sundresses and strappy sandals.

"Where did you get those pants?" Dava cried. "I haven't seen anything like them in years."

Stevie raised her chin and forced herself to meet her cousin's eyes. "I know you're stuck out here in the sticks, Dava, but I'm surprised you haven't heard these are in style."

Dava looked uncertain. "What makes you think so?"

"Because I'm wearing them," Stevie replied coolly, then beat a hasty retreat before anyone could think of a response. She was shaking with anger, and any appetite she may have had when she arrived at the party had deserted her. Needing to get away and regroup but too intimidated to use the back way again, she slipped through the front door and headed down the driveway. She figured nobody would miss her.

It was about nine o'clock, but the sun hadn't completely set yet. One of the dreaded mosquitoes buzzed in her ear. She waved it away and began to ramble down the street, figuring that as long as she kept moving, she might keep the bugs at bay.

The distance between houses surprised her. Most of them were set far back from the main road, secluded by large trees, some even by small orchards. At one point she paused to look between the bars of a wrought iron gate at an old cemetery. She found graveyards fascinating, and she wished fervently that Lisa and Carole could be there to explore it with her.

She wandered a little farther along the road and was thinking of turning back when she noticed she was walking next to a wooden-railed fence. Beyond it was a grassy field with a small pond. *This would be a nice place to keep horses.*

Up ahead, the fence veered out of sight around a bend in the road. As she rounded the corner, her heart leaped

95

with joy. Two horses stood grazing peacefully. One was a gray and the other a bay with two white socks.

Stevie was tempted to reach out and try to coax them closer. She would have loved to give them a pat on the nose and feel their warm breath on her hand. Instead she contented herself with leaning on the top rail and gazing at them. She didn't even mind the mosquitoes.

"You like horses?"

Stevie let out a yip of surprise, which startled the animals. They threw up their heads and snorted, ears pricked in her direction.

The boy standing next to her was tall and thin. He had longish dark hair and deep brown eyes. "I didn't hear you come up," she said a little nervously, suddenly wondering how smart it was to go walking at night in a strange neighborhood without telling anyone where she was going.

"Yeah, I could tell by your reaction," he laughed.

Nice laugh, Stevie thought. "You could have made a noise or something," she said, determined to hide her uneasiness.

"I did, actually, but you were mesmerized. Never seen a horse before?"

"Of course I have," Stevie said scornfully. "In fact, I own one."

"You do? That's great!" He smiled.

Nice smile.

"I own two," he told her.

Is he trying to impress me? Let's see if he really knows anything about horses or if he's only pretending. "Really? What kind? Thoroughbreds? Geldings?"

The boy looked disappointed. "I thought you said you owned your own horse."

"I do."

"Then you should know that a Thoroughbred is a breed of horse, while a gelding is a male horse that's been fixed." He turned away from her. "Good night."

Stevie felt ashamed. She had tried to trick him into revealing himself as a horse fraud, and instead it looked as if she was the pretender. "Wait!" she called and hurried after him. "Look, I'm sorry. I'm from Virginia, and I'm visiting my cousin here, and she pretended to like horses in order to tease me and I fell for it and I felt like a fool, so when you said you had two of your own, I automatically didn't believe you and decided to test you, which was incredibly rude of me and I'm really sorry." Stevie hadn't intended to say that much, but it all came out in an uncontrolled rush.

The boy considered her for a moment, then laughed and held out a hand. "I'm Will."

Really nice laugh. "Stevie," she said, shaking his hand.

"One question. Do all the people in Virginia talk so fast?"

Stevie blushed. "Or so much? No. But I haven't had anyone to talk to in days."

"Would you like to meet my horses?"

Would I! "Are they very far from here? I really shouldn't go much farther without telling my parents."

"How about I bring them to you?" he suggested with a grin.

"You'd do that?"

"I can tell you're suffering from a lack of equine companionship. As a fellow rider, it's practically my duty to help if I can."

Stevie laughed. "Will it take long?"

"Not if they're in a good mood." He winked at her, returned to the fence, and let out a series of low, lilting whistles.

To Stevie's surprise, the two horses that had been grazing lifted their heads and trotted obediently over to where Will waited at the fence. "Stevie, I'd like you to meet Honey and Sugar."

"These are your horses?"

"Yep. Actually, this is my family's farm."

Stevie held out a hand for the animals to sniff. "Honey and Sugar?"

Will looked embarrassed. "I know they're goofy names, but I promised my kid sister she could name them, and that's what she chose."

"Sweet."

"I know," he said with a shrug. "Honey and Sugar."

"Not their names. I think it's sweet that you let her name them." She laughed. "And even sweeter that you kept the names after she did."

He reddened and stared at his shoes.

Before long Stevie found herself describing Pine Hollow Stables; her horse, Belle; and, of course, her Saddle Club friends.

Somewhere during the conversation, Will invited her to sit on one of the horses. "We'll be more comfortable."

Stevie didn't need to be asked twice, and with barely a pause in her story, she slipped onto Honey's back. It was pure heaven. It almost felt like coming home. She had a sudden rush of emotion, and for a moment she was afraid she'd burst into tears in front of her new friend. She had been so miserable and lonely for the last few days, Will's simple act of kindness almost overwhelmed her.

Will talked, too, telling Stevie about life on the farm

and his friends and school, but mostly they talked about horses.

The two of them circled the field, never breaking out of a slow walk, but it was enough.

Finally Stevie knew she had to get back to her family; sooner or later she would be missed. "Thanks, Will. I think you saved my life," she said earnestly. "Or at least my sanity."

Will looked embarrassed. "Any time. If you get trapped at your cousin's house again, feel free to come over."

Stevie hurried back to the party, which was in full swing. The first person she bumped into was Dava, who was chatting with Alex.

"Well, well, Cinderella returns to the ball," snickered Dava, looking down her nose. "Except it looks like the clock has already tolled midnight."

Stevie thought about how disheveled she must look. The humidity had caused her hair to curl riotously, her sleeves were rolled back, her clothes were covered with little hairs, and she was certain she smelled of horses. She smiled blissfully.

"What's with her?" Dava demanded of Alex when Stevie didn't respond to her taunt.

Alex took one look at his sister and knew. "She's found a horse," he said. "You been riding, Stevie?"

"Uh-huh." Stevie couldn't wipe the contented smile off her face.

"Not a chance," Dava declared. "The only horses around here belong to . . ." She frowned and sniffed the air. "You *have* been riding!" she accused Stevie. "Wait until I tell the owners. You are going to be in major trouble!"

The smile left Alex's face. "Cut it out, Dava. Stevie wouldn't ride someone's horse without permission. And what are you, anyway, some kind of professional tattletale?"

Stevie felt a surge of affection for her twin. "It's okay, Alex. As a matter of fact"—she allowed herself a slight smile—"I did have the owner's permission." She turned her back on Dava. "Now, if you'll excuse me, I have an e-mail to write."

Stevie left them with her head held high and a spring in her step. She had taken a bareback moonlit ride on a horse in the company of a handsome stranger. Lisa and Carole were going to have to work hard to top that!

7

"COME ON, YOU lazy thing," Lisa called to Chocolate. "An early morning ride will do you good."

"We're not even going to saddle you," Carole told Berry as she led him through the gate.

The two girls had decided on a prebreakfast bareback ride to watch the sunrise.

Lisa managed to get a hold of her horse. "I wonder how Kate is? It feels kind of strange doing this without her."

Carole slipped the bridle over Berry's head and offered him the bit. "We can do it again tomorrow if she's feeling better."

"You know we hang horse thieves around here,"

Paula said. She was standing in the opening of the barn holding a grooming kit.

Lisa felt herself flush as though she had been caught doing something wrong. "We thought we'd take a ride."

Paula shook her head.

"We can't take a ride?" Carole asked.

"You can do whatever you want," Paula assured them. "But you've picked the wrong time to do it."

Lisa was puzzled. It looked like a beautiful morning to her. "We have?"

"You ought to be going tonight. We're expecting a meteor shower." Paula delivered the news with all the enthusiasm of someone announcing a garbage strike.

"Thanks for the information. We'll be sure to go out tonight then as well," Carole said.

"Two pleasure rides in one day." The wrangler shrugged. "Some people have got the life. It's back to work for me." She trudged off.

Lisa stifled a giggle. "Nice of her to tell us."

Carole was grinning, too. "Come on. We'd better get going or we'll be late getting back for breakfast."

They headed for lookout point, the highest spot on the ranch, knowing from experience that the sunrise from there would be spectacular. On the way, they passed a herd of horses kept for the use of the guests. The girls agreed that watching them grazing in the predawn gave them a sense of tranquillity they missed during the school year back in Willow Creek.

The dawn was everything they could wish for—the mountains turning pink and yellow as the sun rose over the craggy peaks, the air crisp and fresh.

They made it back to the ranch in time for the breakfast feast that Mrs. Devine provided each morning. Helping herself to a second serving of steak and scrambled eggs, Lisa noticed Carole lethargically pushing her food around her plate. "I can't believe you're not hungry," she said. "Early morning rides always make me ravenous."

"I was thinking about Kate. Her mom must be pretty worried if she called the doctor."

Upon returning from their ride they had learned that Kate was not only still running a fever but had been sick to her stomach during the night. Mrs. Devine had left a message for the doctor, but he hadn't returned her call yet. "Moms always worry too much. I'm sure Kate will be back on her feet tomorrow."

Carole pushed her half-eaten breakfast away. "In the meantime, that leaves us on our own today. Got any ideas?"

"Feel up to a little honest work?" Paula asked from her place down the table.

"What did you have in mind?" Carole asked.

"I have to ride out to check on some of the free-range horses to make sure none of them are hurt or sick. Kate mentioned you were studying with a veterinarian. I thought you might find it interesting."

"That would be great, Paula," Carole told her happily. "Thanks for asking."

"Mind if I tag along, too? Lisa asked, not wanting to be left out. "I'll try to keep out from under foot."

"Suit yourself," Paula told her. "See you in a little while."

"Gee, I'm overwhelmed by her enthusiasm," Lisa said, feeling like a third wheel on a bicycle.

"Actually, I think she's warming up," Carole said.

"Don't be hurt, Lisa," Mrs. Devine told her. "A 'suit yourself' coming from Paula is practically an engraved invitation. Carole's right, she must have taken a real liking to you two."

Lisa and Carole helped clean up the breakfast dishes, then decided to quickly check on any new e-mails from Stevie before going out to meet Paula.

"A horseback ride with a boy," Lisa crowed as she read. "Sounds as if things are looking up for Stevie. I'd like to have seen the look on Dava's face when she found out."

Carole raised her eyebrows. "I'd like to see the look on her boyfriend Phil's face when he finds out."

"Nobody's more faithful than Stevie," Lisa declared. "Besides, this thing was probably exactly what she needed to restore her confidence."

"Shall we tell her about our ride this morning?"

"Of course," Lisa said automatically, then had second thoughts. "Just be sure to tell her how cold and wet it was."

"Cold and wet?" Carole protested. "It was beautiful."

"The last time we got happy news from Stevie, it turned out her cousin was playing a nasty joke on her, remember? What if this new relationship turns sour?"

"Hmmm," mumbled Carole. "Good point. There *was* dew on the grass."

"Dew is very wet stuff," Lisa told her with a wink.

Carole nodded. "Very wet."

"And if that morning breeze had kicked up a little more, it definitely could have been cold," added Lisa.

"True," said Carole. "Wet and cold." She broke into a conspiratorial grin. "You're learning fast, Lisa."

"WE ALWAYS KEEP a small herd of horses near the ranch for the use of the guests," Paula explained as they rode.

"But we also have a group of animals that are allowed pretty much the run of our range. Every now and then I need to check on them."

"There they are!" Carole exclaimed.

Lisa followed the direction she was pointing and saw the horses down in a shallow bowl of grassland, grazing peacefully. A movement on the hillside caught her eye. "It's the stallion," she said, awestruck.

The horse stood above the herd on an outcropping of rock, nobly watching over his charges below, eyes and ears alert for the smallest signs of trouble. The wind rippled through his mane and made his long tail flutter as he eyed the newcomers warily.

"He's checking us out," Paula told them in hushed tones. "He knows me, but not you. Let's give him a chance to make up his mind about you."

After a few minutes of intensive staring, the stallion moved off, snatching a quick mouthful of grass here and there as he continued his patrol.

"Guess you guys passed muster," Paula told them, nudging her horse forward. "He's a smart one, that Shot Gun is."

Lisa could hardly believe her ears. Unless she was mistaken, that had sounded suspiciously like a compliment. "Is that his name?"

Paula nodded. "Yep."

"Do they all have names?"

"Nope."

For a moment Lisa thought that was all Paula was going to say.

"Only the special ones," Paula finished by way of explanation.

"What do you carry in your medical bag?" Carole asked after a long silence.

"The usual: antiseptic, gauze, tetanus shots, a couple of tonics. Of course, we can only do remedial first aid out here, but luckily we hardly ever need more. These animals seem to do fine all by themselves."

As soon as they infiltrated the outer ranks of the herd, Paula and Carole started looking for any signs of injury among the members. Lisa felt a twinge of jealousy for their skills. Although she could detect the obvious ailments like a cut or a pronounced limp, it took trained eyes to ferret out the more subtle problems. Paula was obviously experienced at it, and Carole, with her veterinary training, wasn't far behind.

There were times during the day when things seemed touch and go. Some of the horses, especially the ones with foals, were shy about letting the younger girls near. Paula, however, had a strong bond with them. Lisa watched with surprise as time after time the wrangler sweet-talked a mare into letting her rub salve into a wound that was in danger of infection, gave a skittish foal a vitamin tonic, or simply picked stones out of a wary animal's hoof.

Before long both she and Carole had developed great admiration for the usually taciturn woman.

"Okay," Paula said. "We're about finished here."

Lisa held up a hand. "Wait." She reigned to a halt. "Did you hear that?"

The three of them fell silent and listened intently.

"I don't hear anything," Paula said.

"Maybe it was my imagination," Lisa admitted, "but—" At that moment the sound came again: a groaning.

"I hear it," Carole cried.

"Definitely a horse," said Paula. "And it sounds like it's in trouble. Good ears, Lisa."

Lisa felt a surge of pride.

"Could one of the mares be foaling?" Carole asked.

The wrangler shook her head. "I doubt it. Too late in the season. We'd better check it out."

Led by the pitiful noises, it took only a few moments to locate the mare. She was lying on her side, sweating and groaning.

Paula knelt by the horse's head and stroked her lathered neck with gentle hands. "It's okay now, girl. We're gonna take care of you."

The animal lifted her head and looked around at her flanks, then flopped back down.

"What is it?" Lisa asked, concerned.

"Colic," Carole told her calmly. "Did you see the way she was looking at her belly? That's one of the prime symptoms."

Lisa may not have been an expert on horse problems, but even she knew that colic, if untreated, could kill. She knotted her hands together nervously. "Is there anything we can do?"

"You betcha," Paula assured her. "Get that halter off my saddle. We have to get her on her feet, otherwise she'll try to roll and possibly twist an intestine."

Lisa hurried to do as she was told. "What causes this?"

"She probably ate something that didn't agree with her," Paula said, slipping the halter over the animal's head. "And since horses can't throw up, which is what you or I would do, we're gonna have to help her get it through her system. Okay, let's get her up."

The three of them proceeded to pull, push, and prod the reluctant mare to her feet. The horse stood on widespread wobbly legs, head hanging low, periodically moaning.

"Carole, get me that bottle from my bag. The one with the yellow label. We're going to dose her."

The two girls watched anxiously as Paula proceeded to pour the contents of the bottle down the animal's throat. "Hopefully that should take care of it. I'll have to keep her walking for a while, though."

"We can take turns," Lisa offered.

For the first time since they had met, Paula smiled at her. "I'd be obliged if you would."

For the next hour the three of them kept the mare moving continuously. At the slightest pause, the horse attempted to lie down again and roll or to paw at her stomach, but as time passed it happened less and less frequently.

Lisa was taking another turn when Paula called out, "Hold up there. Let's take a good look at her." She came close and ran an expert hand over the animal. "She's stopped sweating, hasn't tried to lie down for a while, no groaning and she dropped some manure. I think we're out of the woods, ladies."

Lisa smiled with relief as Carole straightened a crick out of her back.

"Here's the thing," Paula continued. "There's another animal not far from here. He cut himself pretty bad a week or so ago, and I need to go check on him

111

before dark. Do you think I could leave you here alone?"

The two of them nodded.

"She still needs to be walked for another half hour before you turn her loose."

"Don't worry, Paula," Carole said. "We can handle it. You go ahead."

Paula nodded and mounted up. "Are you sure you can find your way back home?"

"Are you kidding?" Lisa said. "We know this ranch like the back of our hands. We'll see you back at the house."

With a tip of her hat, Paula rode off.

Carole sank back onto the soft grass.

"Hey, it's your turn, lazybones," Lisa chided her.

"Would you mind making a few extra rounds?" Carole pleaded. "I've got a huge headache."

Lisa noticed her friend's hat on the ground. "How long have you had that off?"

Carole shrugged. "Don't know. A while I guess. I lost track."

"You'd better put it back on, then," Lisa urged. "You could get sunstroke, and that's dangerous. As soon as I'm done walking the mare, we'll get you home to rest."

8

LISA WAS TIRED and hungry when they finally arrived at the ranch, but she was elated about having helped the mare. Carole, on the other hand, seemed strangely quiet. Lisa figured that Carole, having worked with the veterinarian at Pine Hollow, had probably seen much more exciting things than a simple case of colic, but to her the afternoon had been a real adventure. Only one thing marred the return journey: About three-quarters of the way home, Chocolate had started to favor one of her legs. She'd asked Paula to look her over before their ride out to view the meteor shower that evening.

The large metal triangle hanging from the porch

113

clanged, announcing it was mealtime. "You girls hurry and wash up now," Mrs. Devine called as they approached the house. "Or there won't be anything left."

Lisa laughed at the idea. Mrs. Devine always made enough food to feed a small army. "How's Kate doing?"

"Not as well as I'd like. The doctor took some blood samples and gave her some medicine, but . . ." Her voice trailed off, and she looked very worried.

"Do you think we could see her for a minute before dinner?"

At first Mrs. Devine looked doubtful, then she seemed to change her mind. "Yes, of course. A quick visit from you might be exactly the thing to cheer her up."

Lisa didn't miss the emphasis on the word *quick*. "We won't take long," she assured her.

"We'll just say hi," Carole concurred.

They hurried down the hall and knocked lightly on Kate's bedroom door.

"Come in."

Lisa poked her head in. "Hi there," she said brightly. When she got closer to the bed, she was taken aback by her friend's pallor and the dark circles under her eyes. "Gosh, you don't look so hot."

"Thanks a lot."

"Nice bedside manner, Lisa," Carole scolded her, then turned to Kate with concern. "How are you doing?"

"I'm okay," Kate told her, waving a hand weakly in the air. "It's only the flu."

Lisa and Carole exchanged worried looks.

"I feel bad about the whole thing, though," she moaned. "You two came all the way out here for some fun, and I had all these things we were going to do, and now I'm stuck in bed. I bet you guys are bored out of your minds. You're never going to want to come back!"

"That's not true," Lisa reassured her. "We're having a great time."

"Not as good as if you were with us, though," Carole added hastily.

Kate looked mollified. "I hear there's a meteor shower tonight. You should go watch it."

"We're going right after sunset," Carole told her.

"We'd better leave now, or your mom won't let us come back," Lisa said, edging toward the door. "Sleep tight."

TO THEIR SURPRISE, Paula was waiting for them when they got to the stables. She had on her usual hangdog expression. "Bad news, Lisa. Chocolate's out of action."

"Her foot?"

Paula nodded. "It's only a bruised frog, but she'll need to rest it for a few days."

Lisa nodded. "You can't be too careful about the bottoms of a horse's feet." She was crestfallen. Outside of being very fond of Chocolate, she had been planning to ride her on tonight's adventure.

"I saddled up Stewball for you instead," Paula said, indicating the waiting horse. "I figured Kate wouldn't be needing him."

Lisa felt her stomach clench. She thought Stewball was a wonderful horse, but his personality was more suited to Stevie than to her. He had always struck her as somewhat mischievous, which was part of his appeal for Stevie. She, on the other hand, preferred an animal that was more solid and reliable. Still, she would have to make the best of it. If she and Carole were going to make it out to the dig in time to view the show, they would have to get moving. "Thanks, Paula, that was nice of you."

"I wasn't busy," Paula grunted. "By the way, I stopped by and checked that mare on the way home. She's fine. You two did a good job." She headed back into the barn. "Have a good ride," she called over her shoulder.

Lisa's spirits were soaring when they set off. It was a little before ten o'clock and the night seemed perfect, the sky clear and cloudless. A soft breeze caressed her face and ruffled the long grass in front of them as they rode. It rippled like the surface of a vast emerald ocean. Earlier in the day she and Carole had agreed to watch the meteor shower from the top of the canyon that overlooked the archaeological dig site. They both felt that the presence of long-dead dinosaurs would lend a primordial feel to the whole event.

They cleared the last of the trees and approached the edge of the cliffs, the light of the moon highlighting the steep rocky walls of the canyon before them.

"I wouldn't want to accidentally ride off the edge," Lisa said a little nervously, looking at the immense drop to the bottom.

"Don't worry, Stewball wouldn't let that happen."

Lisa didn't share her friend's confidence.

The two of them rode along the rim of the canyon for a short distance, searching for the perfect place to view the coming spectacle.

Lisa spotted an outcrop of rock. "Let's tie the horses up and grab a seat," she suggested, sliding easily from Stewball's back. She noticed that Carole seemed to be moving a little slowly, but a sudden flash of light in the

117

sky distracted her from worrying about her friend. "Hurry up, I think it's starting." She untied the blanket from the back of her saddle, then spread it on the ground. She thought of dangling her legs over the edge but chickened out at the last minute. *No sense in taking unnecessary chances.*

Then the meteors began streaking through the sky. At first there were only one or two with long moments between, but after a while they came in greater and greater numbers.

"They look like fireworks that haven't exploded," Lisa said. "Like when they shoot them up on the Fourth of July and you see that streak of light before they burst."

"Uh-huh," Carole said softly at her side.

"Of course, these are coming down, not going up. Hey, shouldn't we be making wishes? Aren't people supposed to wish on falling stars?"

"I guess so," Carole replied quietly.

"Talk about efficient, we could get a whole year's worth of wishes in one night," Lisa said enthusiastically. "What shall we wish for?"

"How about a doctor?" Carole murmured.

Lisa turned and was shocked to find her friend curled up in a small ball. "Carole, what's wrong?"

"I don't feel very good. I think maybe I caught Kate's flu," she mumbled through chattering teeth.

Lisa put a hand on her friend's forehead and recoiled. "You're burning up!" she cried.

To Lisa's horror, Carole began to convulse. Shivering and shaking from the fever, her limbs twitched and spasmed, her eyes rolled back in her head, and she moaned and muttered unintelligibly.

Lisa was extremely frightened, but she reached out and firmly held Carole's head to prevent it from knocking against the ground. Time crawled by with painful slowness; Lisa's heart seemed to pound out each and every passing second. Finally the spasms eased off and Carole fell still. Moving quickly, Lisa stripped off her jacket to make a pillow, gently slipped it under her friend's head, then wrapped the blanket around her.

Carole's eyes fluttered. "What happened?" she said groggily.

"It's all right," Lisa hastened to assure her, forcing herself to speak calmly and soothingly, in the same manner Paula had spoken to the horses that afternoon. "You're sick, but if you go to sleep, when you wake up everything will be fine."

Carole nodded wearily. "Have to sleep now," she

murmured, then went out like a switched-off light-bulb.

Lisa fought off panic. She desperately needed to get help. What first aid she knew wasn't going to be nearly enough in this emergency: Carole needed real medical care. The problem was, there was no way Lisa could get her back to the ranch, which meant she would have to leave Carole there alone while she rode for help.

"Carole, I have to go get help," she whispered softly. "I'm coming back with a doctor, okay? I'll be back soon." She had no way of knowing if her friend could hear her, but she wanted to say the words anyway just in case.

Lisa hurried over to Stewball and mounted, her heart in her throat and her stomach twisting with anxiety. "It's going to be all right, Carole," she called as she rode off into the night. "I promise."

Behind her under the blanket, with only the cold stars to watch over her, Carole lay still as death.

9

LISA DOUBLED BACK the way they had come earlier that night. Her plan was to return to the ranch as fast as possible. As she rode, she was haunted by visions of what might happen to Carole while she was gone. Her friend could have another seizure and swallow her tongue, or a poisonous snake might bite her, or a hungry coyote drawn to the scene by her moans—Lisa couldn't bear to finish the thought. This was truly a nightmare.

At the point in the trail where Lisa was supposed to turn her back to the canyon and ride away from it, she spotted a light in the darkness below. Not trusting her eyes, wondering if it might only be wishful thinking,

121

she blinked and waited until she saw it again. Someone was down at the dig site.

Of course, she thought. *Professor Jackson mentioned they were getting ready to move some of the artifacts to the museum. They're probably working overtime in the cool of the night to do it.* She felt a warm rush of relief. Surely someone would have a cell phone or radio she could use. It would cut the time for help to arrive in half!

Lisa turned Stewball around. Although he seemed somewhat reluctant to comply, she firmly insisted. "I'm the boss here, kiddo."

She couldn't really blame him for not wanting to traverse that steep and narrow trail down to the canyon floor. It had been treacherous enough in broad daylight, but this was an emergency. Trying not to think about the consequences of a fall, she urged Stewball forward. Carefully and painstakingly the courageous horse worked his way downward. Once she felt him slip and her heart lurched, but he quickly recovered and continued on.

By the time they made it to the bottom, Lisa was in a cold sweat, and she figured she had used up every one of the wishes coming to her from that night's meteor shower. At the base of the trail she decided to leave Stewball behind, knowing that with the canyon floor roped off for the dig, it would prove a nasty maze for the horse to try to negotiate by moonlight. She'd actually be able to move faster on foot. The only trouble was there was nothing to tie him to. She knew many cow ponies would ground tie—that was dropping the reins and telling the horse to stay put—but she wasn't sure Stewball was one of them. If he wandered back up the hill without her, she would have to climb back up on foot.

She took the horse by both sides of his bridle and looked him in the eyes. "Stay here, Stewball," she told him firmly. "Wait for me here. Stay." She didn't know if it was necessary to use certain key words, but there was no point in worrying about it—she'd find out soon enough if it worked. Slipping the reins over his head, she dropped them on the ground in front of him. "Stay." Then she backed away around the boulder and ran toward the lights.

Lisa was surprised by the amount of activity in the camp. The pace was definitely more frantic than it had been during the day. A man hurried by her and she tried to get his attention. "Can you help me, please? My friend—" He rushed past, ignoring her completely.

Desperate to get help, Lisa made her way across the site toward the tents. She tried several times to get someone to stop and talk to her, but nobody would stand still long enough for her to explain her situation. She didn't recognize anyone from her last time there, either. She couldn't find Joanne, and Professor Jackson was nowhere in sight.

Eventually she spotted a small knot of adults standing in the light of a Coleman lantern, passing a bottle and laughing. She was determined to make them listen to her this time. "I need help!" she said firmly and clearly as she strode up. "My friend needs a doctor."

All four men looked severely startled to see her there. One of them, a fat man with a big black mustache, stepped forward. "Who are you? What are you doing here?" he said sharply. "This is private property!"

"I'm a friend of Professor Jackson's. I need help. My friend is sick. Can you take me to him?"

Two workers came staggering out of the tent laden down with a large crate. One of them stumbled over a rope, and the box went crashing to the ground.

"You idiot!" screamed the man she had been talking to. "See that you're more careful, or I'll have your hides! Those are priceless."

"Well, not quite priceless," Lisa heard one of the others snicker as they hurried over to check on the contents.

That was when it hit her. These people weren't with the dig, they were poachers. Archaeological thieves, stealing the professor's finds!

She realized at once that she was in serious trouble. If they were criminals, then she was an eyewitness. Slowly, while the men were still focused on the dropped box of dinosaur bones, she began to creep away. She managed to back almost out of the circle of light without drawing their attention, then she slipped on a loose rock and fell heavily to the ground. At once, all eyes were focused on her.

"Get her!" someone shouted.

With a scream, Lisa scrambled to her feet and fled, running as fast as she could, leaping over ropes and rocks. She could hear her pursuers yelling behind her; one man sounded alarmingly close. She risked a glance back over her shoulder and screamed again. A man with a nasty scar across his cheek was reaching out for her. She dodged left and leaped across a pit. Behind her she heard the man fall, hit the ground, and swear harshly. She redoubled her efforts. If she could reach Stewball, she'd have a good chance of escaping. But would he still be there?

The last twenty yards to the big boulder felt like miles, but she finally rounded the corner and her heart jumped. Stewball was standing patiently, exactly where she had left him. "Thank you, thank you, thank you," she gasped, running to his side. She was afraid he might spook and bolt, but she dared not take the time to approach him properly. The horse rolled his eyes and shuffled nervously but stood his ground.

In a flash she was in the saddle, and none too soon. The men charged around the corner, shouting angrily in Spanish. She didn't understand their words, but she understood their intentions. "Go, Stewball, go!" she cried.

As the horse started forward, one of the men dived at him. "Got him!" he shouted.

Lisa looked back to see him clinging desperately to Stewball's tail with both hands.

"No!" she shouted.

She felt the horse lurch beneath her as he kicked out with both hind feet. There was a loud cry of pain, and suddenly they were free, scrambling and stumbling up the path. Within moments Lisa heard the voices behind her receding into the distance. "Atta boy!" she called to the horse.

Heart racing in her chest, Lisa slowed the pinto to a safer pace, working her way back up the steep trail from the canyon floor. Five minutes later she had cleared the top and stopped to get her bearings. The sound of an approaching car engine caught her attention. Not twenty-five yards away, a Jeep rolled to a halt. Filled with relief, she was about to call out when something stopped her. Was it possible that whoever had arrived was not friendly, but actually more poachers?

In the next instant her worst fears were realized.

"Check over there!" someone yelled. "She couldn't have gotten out of here yet."

The thieves had clearly radioed ahead and their colleagues had come to cut her off. Lisa quickly considered her options. She couldn't go directly to the ranch because they were blocking the path. She couldn't go to the left because that would lead them to Carole. Her only choice was to lead them away. *If I can get them to follow me*, she thought, *maybe I can circle around them farther ahead.*

At that moment there was a shout and one of the men pointed in her direction. Without hesitation she whirled Stewball around and urged him into a mad gallop. Traveling at breakneck speeds over unfamiliar ground, at the edge of a sheer cliff in the pitch-black of night, was enormously dangerous, especially on a horse she had never ridden before, but she didn't feel she had a choice. Moments after she took off, she heard the Jeep start up and knew the men were in pursuit.

Lisa didn't dare look back—it was taking every ounce of concentration simply to stay in the saddle. The path she had chosen was getting narrower and narrower, and, to her dismay, there was a steep drop on either side of her. Any hopes she'd harbored about slipping off onto a side trail were dashed.

A moment later Lisa heard the Jeep grind to a stop. Pulling Stewball to a halt, she listened. The men were arguing loudly; apparently the trail was too narrow for the Jeep. For a moment she felt her hopes soar, and then she saw three figures step into the headlights. They were carrying guns.

"Give it up, little girl," one of them called. "There's nowhere to go from there. It's a dead end."

Straining her eyes against the darkness, Lisa scanned the path ahead. She had no idea if they were telling the truth, and she certainly had no reason to believe anything they might say, so she urged Stewball into a fast walk to put some distance between her and the thieves.

Within fifty feet, however, the horse came to a halt and refused to move. Looking in front of her, Lisa felt like bursting into tears. The path simply ended, and all she could see beyond was blackness.

The men followed, slowly moving closer. "Come on,

little girl, we're not going to hurt you. We only want to talk to you."

"Besides, the only way down is the hard way!" one of the others hollered.

They moved at an almost leisurely pace, as though certain of the outcome of the chase.

The sound of their laughter enraged and frightened Lisa. "Leave me alone!" she screamed, tears blurring her vision. "I just want to go home!"

Then, to her complete horror, she felt Stewball lurch beneath her, and the two of them went over the cliff.

10

LISA SCREAMED AS she felt the horse jump. A second later Stewball hit the ground and she was thrown forward, the saddle horn ramming her in the stomach and knocking the wind out of her. She clutched frantically at the knob, trying to keep herself from pitching forward over the horse's neck. Rocks and shale slid all around her, tumbling down the face of the cliff. Stewball gave one more lurch forward and then stood still.

Lisa looked wildly around. To her left was the sheer rocky wall of the cliff, close enough to touch. To her right, a mind-numbing abyss. She risked a cautious look behind and saw a pile of loose rock. With his night vision, Stewball had known what she had not: There was

TRAIL RIDE

an old, virtually unused trail down here. Apparently when she had yelled that she wanted to go home, he had taken her at her word and took the fastest route.

Voices shouted above, reminding Lisa that she was not out of danger yet.

"Did you see that? She jumped!" one of the men was yelling incredulously.

"I never seen nothing like that."

She could hear them approaching the cliff face.

"She didn't jump, she fell."

"Whatever. Is she dead?"

Against the moon, Lisa could make out the vague shape of a head in a hat peering over the edge of the precipice. She pressed back against the cliff wall and held perfectly still, willing Stewball to do the same. The horse's scramble to find footing had carried them a short distance from where they had vanished, so her pursuers were focused on the wrong spot, but one small movement of horse or rider would give them away.

"Of course she's dead, you idiot! Nothing could survive that fall."

"Can you see her?"

"No, I can't see her, you moron, it's dark! She and that horse are probably buried under a pile of rock down there, and I don't have X-ray vision."

131

"We'd better go tell Hatch, then. Problem sort of solved itself, didn't it?"

The voices were fading into the distance. "Did you hear her scream?" were the last words Lisa could make out.

It looked like the poachers were one less thing for her to worry about, but her sigh of relief was cut short as her situation became clear. She was precariously balanced on what appeared to be little more than an old goat trail. She had no idea how far it continued down and no way to go back the way she had come, even if she'd wanted to.

"Kate said you have some mountain pony in you, Stewball," she said, nervously patting his neck. "Guess this is where we find out if that's true."

Having no other options, Lisa gathered her reins loosely in her left hand and took a shameless death grip on the saddle horn with her right before giving the pinto a gentle nudge. It was all up to the animal now. Her life was in his hands.

Stewball moved slowly forward, picking his way cautiously down the precarious path. It seemed to Lisa that he was testing every piece of ground ahead of them before committing his weight to it, which suited her fine. She made no effort to interfere, only doing her best not to throw him off balance. To control her own anxiety, she tried to avoid looking down into the dizzying depths of the shadow-filled canyon. How the horse managed to keep his footing she had no idea. She wasn't sure she could have walked along that path even with her spine pressed tight to the wall, let alone with four feet and a person on her back. They inched along at a painfully slow pace, each and every step life-threatening. Once in a while she would try to look ahead, but mostly she contented herself with sitting quietly, eyes screwed tightly shut, letting the horse take control. When she closed her eyes she saw her friend lying in the cold prairie grass. When she opened them she saw blackness.

Stewball stopped moving. Lisa opened her eyes to see what was the matter, and her heart plummeted to her boots. Part of the trail was gone. Apparently a rock slide had wiped a section of it clean off the cliff face. In the ten-foot gap was a pile of loose rock and shale that would offer no footing.

On the far side of the gap, the path continued for a short distance, then made a sharp right. It headed down a steep grade, then doubled back in their direction about twenty feet below. The area affected by the landslide was substantially narrower on the trail below. In fact, the lower gap looked small enough to jump—if they could only get to it. The immediate problem was the area currently confronting them. The distance across appeared impossible to span.

Doubtfully, Lisa looked behind her. By the light of the moon she could make out the treacherous path the two of them had already traveled to get to where they now stood. She reasoned they were about halfway down, and there was no room on the narrow path to turn around. Her heart thumped painfully against her rib cage as panic mounted. There was no going forward; there was no going back.

Perhaps she and Stewball should stay where they were and wait for help to come in the morning. When she and Carole didn't return to the ranch they would surely be missed. Naturally Mr. Devine would send out a search party. But would Carole be alive by the time they got back to her? Lisa had no way of knowing how sick her friend was, but her condition had certainly appeared very serious. There was no time to wait for a rescue. Lisa was going to have to take action herself.

Stewball shifted his weight uneasily. He was waiting for her decision, and he seemed to be picking up on her fear. If she wasn't careful she would shatter his confidence, and then they truly would be doomed.

Forcing all doubt from her head, she considered her options. There was no way to span the gap in a single jump, but maybe, just maybe, the shale in the middle wasn't as loose as it appeared. If Stewball could find even a little extra foothold, with a lot of luck they might make it to the other side.

Lisa gathered her tattered courage. An inner voice shrieked that what she was about to try was utterly insane, but she refused to listen. Straightening her shoulders, she sucked in a big breath of air and signaled Stewball to step backward. The horse complied, moving cautiously. His second step sent a small river of rocks running down the face of the jagged cliff. To Lisa it seemed like the sound of their falling would never end—a grim reminder of how far it was to the floor of the canyon and safety.

Lisa leaned forward a little. "Stevie swore you could tell what your rider wanted almost before they knew it themselves. So I guess you know what I've got in mind here." Stewball's ears flicked back, indicating he was listening to her. "Look, if you have a better idea, now would be a good time to tell me about it, because otherwise I think we're out of choices. Shall we do this?"

The horse remained stubbornly mute.

"I'm going to take that as a yes."

Lisa had read somewhere that in order for a horse to find courage to jump a scary obstacle, it was necessary for its rider to commit her own heart first. Lisa's heart was definitely on the other side of that obscene gap, waiting to be reclaimed. Before she could lose her nerve, she kicked the horse sharply in the sides, urging him forward with all her will. "Go, go, go!" she yelled.

Stewball responded with a bound that carried him to the edge of the trail, then out into the blackness.

They didn't make it.

For one wild moment Lisa thought they might actually clear the whole distance, but they landed short, hitting the treacherous pile of shattered rocks. Stewball scrambled wildly to find footing where none existed, and it was all Lisa could do to stay in the saddle as he thrashed and fought, sliding inexorably downward.

"No!" she screamed helplessly as they neared the point where they would be swept past the lower trail and over the edge. Her cry was echoed by a desperate whinny from Stewball, who miraculously came up with a little more power. With one last mighty surge forward, he managed to carry the two of them back onto firm ground.

"Oh, you amazing horse!" Lisa cried, slapping his neck heartily. She was trembling from head to toe, and Stewball was huffing from his tremendous effort.

She felt a warm trickling on her chin, and when she reached up to wipe at it, her hand came away smeared with blood. During the struggle to reach the other side of the trail she had bitten her lip. She laughed, enjoying the salty taste of the blood. It reminded her that she was still alive.

Studying her new situation, however, Lisa realized that something was terribly wrong. After sliding down the mountain twenty feet, Stewball had managed to leap forward onto the lower section of the trail, saving them from plunging over the cliff, but now they were facing the wrong direction. If they went forward they'd only reach a hairpin turn to the left that would take them back to the upper gap. The descending trail was behind them, and the path in front was too narrow to turn around on.

She twisted in the saddle to look over her shoulder. The gap down here was, indeed, narrower, and Stewball could traverse it fairly easily—if he was facing the right direction. No horse could jump it backward, and even if he could there was no way he could negotiate that ridiculously tiny trail all the way down to the bottom if he was moving backward. Sooner or later he would put a foot down wrong and it would be all over for both of them. Not to mention for Carole.

Lisa suddenly realized she was the only one who knew where to find the stricken girl. If she and Stewball didn't make it, the odds seemed good that Carole wouldn't, either.

Okay, Lisa, think, think, think, think!

She continued looking around, trying to sift substance from shadow, scanning for any place that showed the slightest widening in the trail. Then she spotted it, or at least she thought she did. Just before the hairpin turn leading upward, there was a rocky outcropping that formed an overhang. It looked like there might be a small indentation under it. *It probably won't be much, but it's the best chance we've got right now.* Gently she urged Stewball forward.

There was indeed a small hollowed-out chunk in the wall, and the trail did widen a little, but certainly not enough to allow a horse to make a conventional turn.

If it weren't for bad luck we'd have no luck at all, Lisa thought.

Lisa chewed her sore lip in frustration. There had to be something she could do, some way for her to take advantage of this slight cavity. How could Stewball make a turn without putting his front feet down?

Suddenly she heard an echo of Kate's voice in her head. *"Out here we call that a rollback."* Lisa's eyes grew wide as she remembered how the horse had pivoted on his hindquarters to face in the completely opposite direction.

The voices continued in her head, and she heard herself say, *"It was like Stewball did it all on his own."*

"He almost did. He's been doing those moves so long, all I had to do was give him a hint of what I wanted."

Her heart raced. If she could get Stewball to do one of those turns, they might still have a chance of getting out of this nightmare with their skins intact. She was sure that if he only knew what she wanted, he would be glad to oblige. Unfortunately, she wasn't sure how to cue the pinto.

Once again she replayed the scene in her mind, focusing on Kate's actions. There had been a subtle shift of the girl's weight deeper into the saddle, and she had lifted the reins toward her right shoulder at least ten inches higher than the normal riding position. Lisa was sure of that much. All that remained was a leg cue. Was it supposed to be in front of the girth or toward the back?

Lisa became aware that time was slipping away, and, with it, Carole's chances of survival. She had no choice but to try—and hope Stewball really was psychic enough to figure out what she wanted.

"All right, boy," she told him. "My money's on you. Now, rollback," she instructed, giving him all the cues she had.

Almost like magic Lisa found herself facing the opposite direction. She blinked in disbelief. It had been so easy!

"You are too much," she crooned to the little horse with a choke in her voice. Stewball nodded his head as if in agreement. For the first time in many hours, Lisa heard herself laugh. It felt good. "Let's keep moving, pardner. After that last jump, this one is cake."

It was. The horse cleared the narrow river of shale with room to spare.

Hoping they had come through the worst of things, Lisa guided her mount forward. For a while they made steady progress, the floor of the canyon growing ever closer with each shuffling step. Then, about forty feet above the flatlands, the trail really came to an end.

Lisa peered down and saw that the wall of the cliff was sheered away and the rest of the precious ledge they had been so painstakingly working their way down was lying at the bottom of the gorge in large rocky pieces.

The angle of the slope to the bottom was hideously steep, perhaps fifty degrees at its worst. It would be easier to ride straight down the face of a pyramid. No horse she knew had a chance of getting to the bottom in one piece on his own, let alone with a rider on his back.

Maybe if I went down by myself I could slide on my butt. Then I could walk to the ranch and send help back for Stewball and Carole.

She had a sudden vision of herself losing her footing and cartwheeling down the mountain head over heels, ending in a heap at the bottom with a broken neck. At the very least she would break a leg, and that wouldn't do anybody any good.

Once more she would have to place her trust in her horse. "What do you say, fella? Are you game for one last roll of the dice?"

Stewball shifted back and forth under her. She could tell he was tired. The strain of walking down such a narrow and steep trail had taken a serious toll on his strength, but she also knew that he was her only hope of getting to the bottom in one piece.

She gently caressed his lathered shoulder. "I know you can do it, boy," she told him solemnly. "Do it for me and Carole, okay?" Mustering what remained of her courage, Lisa closed her eyes, muttered a prayer, and urged the sturdy little pinto over the edge.

The horse dropped out from under her and Lisa thought she would come out of the saddle for sure.

Stewball connected with the earth at an angle that whiplashed her in the opposite direction. She desperately flailed her right arm backward to check her forward momentum and managed to retain her seat. The horse went bounding toward the bottom. He took huge leaps, drawing his powerful hindquarters under him as he struggled to maintain balance in what seemed to be nothing more than a controlled fall.

The ground raced at Lisa with a strange combination of alarming speed and agonizing slowness. Every gut-wrenching lurch threatened to fling her into the air over her straining mount's head, but time and again she gritted it out, teeth clenched tightly, relying completely on instinct and the will to survive and see this monumental task through to the end.

They were almost at the bottom when she felt her overly taxed leg muscles give out. Not even her white-knuckled grip on the saddle horn could save her. The best she could manage was to throw herself sideways to avoid doing a complete cartwheel over the top of the horse as he continued to plunge downward.

She hit the earth with bone-jarring impact. Searing pain ripped through her shoulder. She slipped, rolled, and skidded the rest of the way to the bottom, dragging a small avalanche of rocks and debris with her. At some point she felt her head collide with a rock and everything went black.

Sometime later she woke up, facedown in the dirt. It took a while before she could muster enough strength to roll over and lift her face to the night sky. Her breath coming in ragged gasps, she struggled to stay conscious. Gingerly she began to check herself out. Every inch of her body was in pain, but she was fairly certain that nothing was broken. She forced herself to her knees, the world swimming before her eyes, and promptly threw up.

Finally, when the violent stomach contractions had subsided and she could once again draw little gasps of cool air, she climbed wearily to her feet and looked around. Stewball was standing not far from her. She staggered over and threw grateful arms around his neck, bursting into tears. Before she knew it she was crying almost hysterically against him. Between racking sobs, she heard herself muttering praises of undying gratitude. Stewball seemed to take it all in stride.

Eventually she managed to pull herself together enough to once more climb into the saddle, shaking with shock and muscles like jelly. With utter weariness she picked up the reins and slumped forward in the saddle. She had no idea in what direction the Bar None lay, but she wasn't worried about it.

"Take me home, Stewball," she murmured into his dirt-encrusted mane.

Stewball did as he was told.

11

STEVIE THOUGHT SHE was going to die. At the very least, she was on the verge of a major breakdown.

She had endured an entire day of hanging out with long-lost relatives who, unfortunately, wouldn't stay that way. She couldn't begin to remember all the names of the people to whom she had been introduced. After a while she'd stopped trying and simply did her best to be polite. "Nice to meet you." "My pleasure." "Thank you very much."

Then there was the never-ending rehearsal dinner, a huge feast at one of the best local restaurants, where the food and the wine had flowed nonstop and the conversations had gone on and on and on.

"Is that your brother?"

"Yes, we're twins."

"Fraternal or identical?"

Gee, since he's a boy and I'm a girl . . .

"Remember me, honey? I used to powder your behind when you were a baby."

Great. Like I could remember that, or would even want to.

Dressed in their best, the guests flitted like colorful birds from one table to another. Stevie had tried to be social. She chatted dutifully with anyone who addressed her, but every conversation sounded the same.

"Who do you belong to?"

She would point out her mom and dad and explain their connection with the bride.

"How nice. Are you enjoying yourself?"

"Yes, thank you."

"You look very pretty in that outfit."

"Thank you." Actually, she loathed her clothes: a knee-length, bottle green velvet skirt with matching short jacket and an awful taffeta chartreuse cummerbund.

Next would come an awkward silence as the adult of the moment searched around for something else to say. "What do you want to be when you grow up?"

"I want to do something with horses," she would tell them seriously, hoping someone in the party might actually like riding. But invariably her answer was met with polite smiles of disinterest.

"Oh, horses. How nice, dear."

Then they would excuse themselves.

Stevie figured they were going to find someone more interesting to talk to. She didn't seem to have anything in common with anyone.

By the end of the evening she was desperate to get back to the hotel and tuck herself in bed. The sooner this day was over, the sooner the next one would start, bringing her family's departure for home that much closer.

She checked her watch for the millionth time. Had the hands even moved? She held it to her ear to see if it was still running. Unfortunately, it was.

Finally, to Stevie's immense relief, people started to leave.

"Honey, get your coat. We're going now," her mother told her.

Stevie's heart leaped. If they hurried, she'd still have time to catch one of her favorite shows on television back at the hotel.

"The Sinclairs have invited us back to their house so we can go on talking," her mom continued. "Isn't that nice?"

Stevie was speechless with dismay.

An hour later she was absolutely at the end of her

rope. Avoiding Dava in the house became a full-time job. She finally found refuge in an upstairs bedroom and sat staring out the window. The memory of Honey and Sugar beckoned. They were right there, just beyond the trees. She had to get away. She went in search of her mother.

"Mom, I'm going for a walk, okay?"

Her mother looked out the window at the periodic bright streaks that pierced the darkness and frowned at the murmur of distant thunder. "I don't know, Stevie. It's getting pretty late, and the weather . . ."

"Please, Mom, I don't think it's going to rain. I won't go far and I won't be long, but I have to get out of here for a little while. Please!"

Maybe it was the note of desperation in her voice, or maybe it was because her mother realized how hard Stevie had tried, all day, to make her proud. At last, her mother relented. "All right, go ahead. You've earned a little respite."

Stevie felt a rush of relief. "Thanks, Mom," she said, kissing her on the cheek.

Her mother looked pleased. "Not too long, though. Tomorrow's the big day, and we all need to get some rest."

Stevie nodded her agreement even as she fled. The instant she closed the front door behind her she felt better.

She checked her watch. *Mom's right, it is getting late. There's no way Will will be around, but I bet he wouldn't mind if I just looked at his horses.*

She hurried down the road as fast as her new shoes would let her. Every now and then another streak of lightning would flare, followed by thunder washing across the distance like an incoming wave. *I feel like I'm in a science-fiction movie. Any moment now the carrot creature will leap out and try to kill me!* Stevie laughed at her outrageous imagination. Nonetheless, she didn't linger as she passed the spooky old cemetery.

In a few minutes she was at the paddock, looking around eagerly for the horses. Her spirits fell when she didn't see them. *Maybe they put them in the barn because of the weather. Animals can get very skittish during storms.*

She was about to give up and go home when she got an idea. Pursing her lips, she whistled, doing her best to imitate the tune Will had used to call the horses.

To her delight she heard an answering whinny. Apparently the animals were over the hill just out of her sight. She whistled again and waited hopefully. Her patience was rewarded as Honey trotted into view.

"Hey, beautiful," she called, holding out a hand. "Come here, sweety."

Honey hesitated at the top of the rise.

Stevie whistled again softly, careful not to make any sudden moves.

Honey came toward her and stopped a few feet from the fence, still tantalizingly out of reach. The horse nickered and looked back over its shoulder in the direction from which it had come.

"Where's Sugar?" Stevie asked, keeping her arm outstretched.

Honey pawed the ground.

To Stevie's experienced eye, the horse looked agitated. "Don't be scared," she said in her most reassuring voice. "The storm won't hurt you."

Honey came toward the fence, then circled around and stopped, looking back over the hill, focusing on the distance and scuffing the grass again.

Stevie frowned. Where was Sugar? Why would Will only take one of the animals in? It didn't make sense.

Without thinking about what she was doing, she slipped through the rails into the paddock. She felt a seam in her skirt give way as she went, and when she got to the other side the heels of her new pumps sank into the soft ground. *Uh-oh, Mom's not going to be happy about this.*

Up close, Honey's agitation was even more obvious than before. Stevie tried to get close enough to give her a comforting pat, but the animal would have none of it, shying away and moving farther up the hill. Again Stevie approached, and again Honey retreated a few feet, stopping to snort and paw at the grass.

Stevie had never seen a horse act quite like this and wasn't sure what to make of it. "What's wrong, girl?"

As if in answer, the mare trotted away, this time out of sight down the other side of the hill.

Stevie was perplexed. Curiosity got the better of her and she walked over the rise to see what the animal was up to. To her surprise and delight, she immediately spotted Sugar standing by the edge of the pond with her head bowed. Honey was beside her.

"Well, where have you been?" she asked. She made her way down, the ground sucking at her shoes with each step. "Feeling antisocial?"

This time Honey didn't try to avoid her touch, but snorted loudly.

"Take it easy, girl."

Not wanting Sugar to feel neglected, Stevie began

to stroke her chest. "Hi there, sleepyhead. Too tired to come and say hello to me?" she chided.

The animal shivered. Strangely, Stevie got the impression it was with fear and not with pleasure.

She frowned. Sugar's coat felt wet beneath her fingers. As she pulled her hand away, a flash of lightning illuminated the night.

Stevie screamed. Her hand was covered in blood. Startled, she staggered back a step, her heel caught in the ground, and she sat down hard on her backside. She scrambled to her feet, overwhelmed with concern. Sugar was hurt. She needed to find out how badly.

Questions raced through her mind. *Has the blood flow stopped or is she still bleeding? Is an artery involved? How long ago did this happen?*

Murmuring words of comfort, she moved closer, then crouched down, trying to get a look at how bad the situation was. The darkness hampered her vision. With the utmost gentleness she began to run her hands over the mare. Her fingers glided from the horse's chest down her front leg, looking for the wound. She found it, high on the inside of the left foreleg—a ragged cut that was not only still bleeding but was actually pulsing blood.

It was clearly a major injury, and from the way Sugar

was hanging her head, Stevie had to assume the worst. It had happened a while ago.

She tried not to panic. She knew she had to keep her wits about her. There was no time to run for help. If she didn't slow the bleeding, Sugar might die.

I need to make a tourniquet.

Her fingers trembled as she struggled to undo the clasp on her cummerbund. Finally it came loose. She was about to tie it over the wound but hesitated. There was no way the slippery taffeta was going to bind the gash tight enough to do the job. She would need added pressure to stem the blood flow, especially if she planned on walking the animal back to the farmhouse. She placed her thumb three inches above the gash, pressing hard on the artery. The blood flow stopped. Unfortunately, there was no way she could walk all the way back to the barn in that position.

If only Carole were here, she thought. *She'd know what to do. But Carole is out West with nothing more serious to worry about than where to go on her next trail ride.*

Stevie's mind conjured up a wistful picture of her Saddle Club friends as she had last seen them on the ranch—her, Lisa, Carole, Kate, and Christine laughing and joking under sunny skies.

Her mind seized on something. *Christine Lonetree.*

During the visits they had shared, Christine had taught the girls all manner of interesting lore from her American Indian heritage. One of them had been a simple emergency technique to slow bleeding.

Relinquishing her hold on Sugar's leg, Stevie stumbled toward the pond. Her shoes hampered her even worse in the soft mud by the edge, so she kicked them off impatiently and got down on her hands and knees, her fingers groping through the silt and shallow water. "Come on, come on, come on," she muttered. Finally she found what she was looking for. She pulled out a smooth round stone, which glistened wetly by the light of the moon.

"Perfect!"

She scrambled back to the injured horse and grabbed her cummerbund. Quickly she rolled the stone into the center, then, pressing it against the artery above the wound, tied it tightly into place. The rock would maintain direct pressure and stem the flow of blood almost as well as if she were holding it with her thumb.

She double-checked to make sure the tourniquet was as tight as she could make it, then climbed to her feet. "All right, Sugar, let's get you home."

Easier said than done. The mare was lethargic from

shock and blood loss and was reluctant to move. For a few nasty moments Stevie didn't think she was going to be able to get her going, then Honey came to the rescue. With a sympathetic nicker and a few insistent nudges, she urged her friend into a slow walk.

To Stevie, who worried and fretted with every step and passing minute, the trip back to the main house seemed to last forever. Finally they made it into the soft steady glow of the porch light.

She quickly ran up the steps and started pounding on the door and ringing the bell. It didn't take long before she heard the sound of feet hurrying down a staircase.

The door flew open and a man, hair disheveled and still trying to tie his bathrobe closed, looked at her with surprise. "Who are you?" he demanded angrily. "What do you mean waking us up at this time of night?"

Stevie guessed that this was Will's father. Unfortunately she had never asked Will his last name, so she didn't know how to address him. "Please, sir, it's your horse. She must have been spooked by the storm and run into something. She's gashed open her leg and I think it's pretty bad."

"Honey?" he said, peering past her into the night.

Stevie shook her head. "No, it's Sugar. You have to call the vet," she told him frantically. "I think she's lost a lot of blood."

"Dad, who is it?" a sleepy voice called from inside the house.

Stevie instantly recognized it. "It's Stevie, Will!" she yelled past his father. "Sugar's hurt!"

That was all it took. In a flash the boy was downstairs. A moment later all three of them were racing outside.

Will's father took one look at the horse and immediately went back inside to call the veterinarian. While he was gone, Stevie and Will coaxed the mare into the barn.

When Will's father returned, he noticed Stevie's makeshift tourniquet. He looked at it curiously, and Stevie hastened to explain why she had put it there.

"I've never heard of such a thing," he admitted. "But I think you might have saved Sugar's life."

Stevie flushed with the praise.

The animal doctor arrived shortly after and took charge of the mare.

Stevie knew she had been away from the party far too long and that her parents were probably worrying about her, but she couldn't leave until she heard the prognosis.

Finally the vet told them that Sugar was going to be fine. "She lost a lot of blood, but someone got to her just in time."

Will's father thanked Stevie profusely and then told his son to see her safely home.

On the short trip back to her cousin's house, Will thanked her over and over again. "I know you really wanted to go out West with your friends," he said, "but I'm sure glad you came here instead. If you hadn't, Sugar would have died."

Stevie mulled this over in her head. Missing the trip to the Bar None had devastated her, but if she weighed that against saving a horse's life, the price was well worth it.

With a whole new outlook on the trip, Stevie led the way into the house.

The first person to spot her was Dava, whose eyes went wide with shock and amusement. "Stevie, look at yourself! What have you been up to?" She laughed. "You look like someone dragged you backward through a bush."

Stevie had completely forgotten about her appearance. She glanced down and saw with dismay the torn remnants of her dinner outfit and her mud-covered, shoeless feet.

"There was an accident," she said with quiet dignity. "I had to help."

Dava's scathing laugh rang around the room. "The only accident I see is you," she crowed. "You're a walking disaster!"

"Shut up, Dava!" Alex said, pushing his cousin aside. He looked at Stevie with concern. "You okay?"

After the drama of the last hour, the compassion in his eyes almost made her cry. She nodded mutely.

"The horse okay?"

Stevie's heart soared. Her brother knew her so well. "She's going to be fine."

The two of them shared a moment that only twins could: an almost psychic connection. They had their differences, but their bond would always be unbreakable.

Will stepped into the room and his eyes widened as he spotted Dava. "*You're* Stevie's cousin?"

"W-Will?" Dava stuttered.

"No wonder you had to get out of here," Will murmured to Stevie.

Stevie's head swam. Dava and Will knew each other!

"For your information, Dava," Will continued, his voice filled with contempt, "Stevie just saved my horse's life!"

Dava's mouth opened and shut a few times. "How nice," she finally said.

"Awww, girls," Will muttered contemptuously. Then he quickly turned to Stevie. "Not you, of course. You're the best!"

The absolute crestfallen look on Dava's face was almost as good as the compliment from Will.

At that moment, Stevie's mother appeared in the kitchen doorway, gawking at her daughter. "What in the world . . ."

Stevie straightened her shoulders and went to explain things to her parents. After what she'd just been through, she could face anything.

12

LISA WOKE THE next morning alone in the bunkhouse. She flexed her legs and arms and immediately regretted it. She was sore from head to toe. With a sigh, she lay back in bed and replayed the events of the night before.

She vividly recalled the harrowing ride to get help for Carole, but after her slide down the last part of the cliff, her memory was spotty.

She remembered relying completely on Stewball to see her home, and he had not failed her. There had been a huge outcry when she had ridden in, and someone helped her down, yelling for help.

They had tried to fuss over her but she had insisted

on telling them all about Carole and the thieves at the dig site before letting them clean her face and lacerated hands.

Mr. Devine called for the doctor and sheriff, then hurriedly packed the truck with blankets and a medical kit.

Despite Mrs. Devine's protests, Lisa climbed in the truck, refusing to come out, insisting that the rescue would go faster if she accompanied Mr. Devine back to the site. No amount of cajoling would change her mind, and faced with her implacable attitude, they had finally agreed. It was only as they were pulling out that she remembered the valiant little horse that had seen her this far.

"Paula!" she yelled out the window.

Instantly the wrangler was at the truck door.

"Stewball. You have to take care of Stewball," she told her. "He saved my life!"

Paula assured her that she was already looking after him and she would stay with him all night if he needed it.

The bumpy ride up to the cliff was something of a blur, but Lisa remembered leaping from the vehicle as soon as it had stopped and sprinting to where she had left Carole. To her immense relief her friend was alive and relatively aware, though groggy and still feverish. Even as they were moving her gently into the cab of the truck, the helicopters from the sheriff's department were buzzing overhead on their way to corral the thieves.

By the time they had made the journey back to the ranch, the doctor was there waiting for them and immediately took Carole into the guest room for examination.

"Rocky Mountain spotted fever," he announced when he returned. "I got Kate's blood tests back earlier this evening, and this young lady has the same symptoms. Of course, I can't be absolutely certain until I do some lab tests, but I'm not taking any chances. I've already started Kate on tetracycline, and I'm going to do the same for Carole."

Lisa's heart had contracted with fear. "Spotted fever! Is that deadly?" she asked, trying to keep her voice steady.

The doctor looked at her gravely. "If left untreated it can have severe consequences: partial paralysis of the lower extremities, gangrene leading to possible amputation, hearing loss, possible movement and language disorders."

Lisa realized she must have looked alarmed, because he had placed a comforting hand on her shoulder. "Don't worry, we caught them both in time. You say Carole suffered a seizure this evening?"

162

Lisa nodded.

He nodded his head knowingly. "That's rare. Only about ten percent of victims have that reaction, but it does happen. Good thing for her you were there."

As the doctor checked Lisa out, cleaning and disinfecting her wounds, he questioned her closely about where they had gone and what they had done since arriving at the ranch.

She filled him in to the best of her ability and was surprised to find him smiling when she finished.

"You're making me jealous," he said. "Next time you girls come to visit, I'd sure appreciate an invitation to tag along."

Lisa smiled, too, in spite of her aches and pains.

"Here's my thinking. . . . Rocky Mountain spotted fever is carried by ticks and transmitted through their bite."

Lisa had a sudden flashback to both Kate and Carole scratching their arms and legs over the last few days.

"Since no one else around these parts has complained of the same symptoms," he continued, "I think we can be fairly certain you girls came in contact with it at that pond. That means it's now officially off-limits. Sorry."

Later Mrs. Devine made Lisa a bowl of hot soup and tucked her into bed. The bunkhouse, missing both Kate and Carole, had seemed lonely and big, and Lisa had been sure she would never be able to fall asleep. She was out almost before her head touched the pillow.

Now it was morning and, by the look of the sun, well into it. *I've probably missed breakfast, but maybe I can scrounge something from the kitchen. I'm starving!*

Crawling painfully out of bed, Lisa was forced to put on some of the new clothes her mom had bought because everything else was dirty. The clothes she had worn the night before were downright unsalvageable. She held up the jeans. Her slide down the cliff had really destroyed them—they were torn at the knees and stained with ground-in dirt and blood. The shirt was even worse—sleeves practically ripped from the shoulders, pockets torn off, the front in tatters, and several buttons missing.

She tossed the jeans in the trash and was about to do the same thing with the shirt when she changed her mind and returned it to her suitcase. It would make an interesting memento of the trip.

She limped to the main house, her body protesting every step.

There was nobody around when she got there, so she decided to check on Carole and Kate before looking for food. She didn't knock, in case they were sleeping, but instead eased the bedroom door open quietly and peeked inside.

"Lisa," Carole called to her. "My hero!"

Lisa felt herself blush.

"Come in," Kate invited, propping herself up against a cushion of several pillows.

"How are you two doing?" Lisa asked, closing the door behind her.

Kate made a face and held up her hands. They were covered with red splotches sprinkled with tiny purple dots. "Something for Carole to look forward to," she said ruefully.

Lisa perched on the edge of the bed. "Good thing the prom is a long time away. You might have a hard time getting a date looking like that."

Carole and Kate exchanged looks and burst out laughing. "Have you looked in the mirror this morning?" Carole asked her.

"No."

"Go on, take a peek," Kate urged.

Lisa got up and moved to the vanity mirror. The image it reflected took her completely by surprise. Her lip was swollen and purple where she had bitten it, her chin and the tip of her nose showed nasty red scratches from sliding facedown in the dirt, and she had a shiner to beat all shiners encircling her right eye. She touched it tentatively and winced. "I look like I was in a boxing match!"

"I'd say none of us in this room is prom material," Carole laughed.

"At least you didn't catch this plague," Kate said. "Something to be thankful for."

Lisa smiled wearily. "True."

"I have a lot more than that to be thankful for," Carole said solemnly. "Thank you, Lisa. You saved my life."

Embarrassed, Lisa shrugged. "You would have done the same for me."

"I'm not sure I could have," Carole told her. "Have you seen this?" She pulled something out from under her pillow. "Paula showed it to me this morning."

Lisa went to the bed and took the object from her hand. It was a Polaroid photograph of the face of a cliff. Lisa shrugged. "So?"

"Lisa," Carole said quietly, "that's what you rode down last night."

Lisa was totally stunned. She looked at the picture again, taking in the absurd steepness of the terrain and the teeny tiny trail she now remembered so vividly working her way down. She swallowed hard. "Yeah, well, Stewball did most of the work."

Carole, with tears in her eyes, opened her arms wide. Lisa gave her a big hug, feeling infinitely grateful that the two of them had both made it through the night.

"What about me?" Kate demanded from the other bed.

Lisa laughed and went to hug her, too. The three of them chatted for a little while longer, and then Lisa left them alone to sleep and recuperate while she went in search of food.

Mrs. Devine was in the kitchen, and the minute Lisa showed herself she was enfolded in another warm embrace.

"Good morning, sweetheart," Mrs. Devine gushed. "After what you went through last night, I thought you should sleep as long as you wanted this morning."

"Thanks, Mrs. Devine," she said, settling herself in a chair. "Could I have a couple of pieces of toast?" she asked hopefully. "I can make it myself."

To her amazement Mrs. Devine looked like she was going to burst into tears. "A couple of pieces of toast?" she cried. "After riding down a cliff in the middle of the night to save your friend? When I saw that photograph my heart nearly stopped."

I guess Paula has been making the rounds this morning. I hope she didn't show the picture to the whole ranch.

"It's okay, Mrs. Devine. It's over now."

"You must be starving," she said, wiping her eyes on her apron. "I saved you some breakfast. Ham and eggs and cottage fries." She pulled a heaping plate out of the oven and presented it to Lisa.

"Wow. Thanks, Mrs. Devine," Lisa said gratefully. Her mouth watered as she picked up her fork. "It looks wonderful."

Mrs. Devine smiled happily. "I baked you a fresh batch of biscuits, too. No cowboy leaves home without biscuits in her belly."

Lisa smiled. She remembered Kate's thoughts on biscuits, but it didn't stop her from slathering them with fresh honey and filling herself until she thought she would burst. She would have stopped sooner, but the more she ate the happier Mrs. Devine seemed to look.

While she was eating, Lisa wondered what would happen next. The events of the night before all seemed sort of unreal now, but what was undeniable was the fact that both her friends were confined to bed for the rest of their stay. What was she going to do on her own? She could hang out with Paula, but the woman wasn't exactly a barrel of laughs. Certainly not when compared to Carole, Kate, or Stevie.

Mrs. Devine interrupted her thoughts. "Lisa, there's someone here to see you."

"Really?" she asked, surprised. "Who?"

Her question was answered when Professor Jackson poked his head through the kitchen door. "May I come in?"

Lisa almost knocked her glass of milk over in her rush to rise to her feet. "Of course, Professor."

Professor Jackson crossed the room and took hold of her hand. "Lisa, I can't thank you enough for what you did last night."

"Did they catch the thieves?" In her concern for Carole she had almost forgotten about the attempt to loot the dig site.

"They did," Professor Jackson assured her.

"How much did they get away with?" The idea that those horrible people would be selling the professor's hard-earned fossils really made her mad. Especially after they had practically killed her to get them.

"Not much at all," he told her. "Several of the crooks were very happy to turn on their employer in exchange for more lenient sentences. As a result we recovered almost everything they took."

Lisa was gratified. "I'm glad. How did they get there without the guards being alerted, anyhow?"

The professor looked chagrined. "Apparently I was outbid. They bribed the guards to look the other way."

Lisa shook her head in disbelief.

"Lisa," the professor continued softly. "You do realize that you saved hundreds of irreplaceable artifacts, worth millions of dollars, from disappearing into the black market, don't you?"

Lisa didn't want to disappoint him, but she felt she had to be honest. "I was only trying to save Carole," she confessed. "I sort of stumbled on the other stuff."

The professor reached out, held her chin in his hand, and looked her in the eyes. "My dear girl. I've heard what you did, and I saw where you went. You're amazing. Really amazing."

What did Paula do? Publish the picture in the newspaper?

"How can I possibly thank you?" he asked.

Lisa broke into a smile as an idea came to her head. For the rest of her vacation, Kate and Carole would be out of commission. Maybe she could use the time to learn something new. "Professor," she said slowly, "I'm really fascinated by your dinosaurs. Is there anything I could do to help?"

Professor Jackson smiled broadly, his eyes sparkling. "Oh, my dear . . . funny you should ask. We made a most remarkable discovery only yesterday, and we certainly could use some extra help excavating it.

"You could?"

"Absolutely. Do you know anything about Triceratops?"

13

FINALLY, after what seemed like a very long time, The Saddle Club was back together again.

"It's so nice not to look like a plague victim anymore," Carole said, examining herself in her bedroom mirror. "I finished all my medication today."

"It's too bad, though, that Stevie will never get to see the pond," Lisa said wistfully. "That was an amazing day."

"And this is an amazing souvenir," Stevie told her, looking at a dinosaur tooth that Professor Jackson had given to Lisa. "I can't believe he let you keep it."

"By the end of our stay, the professor told me he would be pleased to work with me any time," she said proudly. "He even told me how to go about applying for an assignment with him when I get to college."

"That's a long way off yet," Stevie reminded her.

Carole clucked her tongue. "It's never too soon to begin planning for your future. But I have to admit, I thought you wanted to do something with horses, Lisa."

"I'm not so sure."

"What?" Stevie cried with consternation.

Lisa laughed. "Take it easy. You know I love horses, and I can't imagine not being involved with them somehow for the rest of my life." She hesitated. "I'm just not sure that they're going to be my career. That dinosaur dig was really fascinating!"

"Sounds like the two of you had the greatest summer of your lives," Stevie moped. "I always miss out on the good stuff."

"Stevie!" Lisa cried. "There's nothing good about having Rocky Mountain spotted fever, and there's nothing fun about riding down a cliff in the dark, wondering if your friend will still be alive when, and if, you manage to return!"

"By the way, the picture of that cliff sent chills down my spine," Stevie told her. "I can hardly believe you could get a horse to go down that thing."

"Stewball is an exceptional horse," Lisa said quietly. "You were right about him all along."

Stevie leaned back in a chair and propped her feet up on the bed. "Yeah, I've got good instincts when it comes to horses," she admitted. She grew serious. "He wasn't hurt or anything, right?"

"I was the one who was trashed," said Lisa. "Outside of a skinned knee and a few little nicks and cuts around his ankles from the loose rocks, he was raring to go the next morning. You'd have thought he'd had the time of his life," she laughed. "It was nice of Paula to ride out and take that photo for me."

"That was some front-page headline that ran with it, too," Carole chuckled.

" 'Girl Foils Thieves in Daring Midnight Ride,' " Stevie quoted. "Thanks for bringing me a copy, Carole."

"No problem."

"I can't believe Paula actually submitted it to the newspaper," Lisa grumbled.

"Sounds like she really warmed up to you two by the end of the visit," Stevie said.

"I can't blame her for not liking us at first, not after Kate built us up like that," Carole said. "You know, Paula may not be the most sociable person in the world, but she sure does know about horses."

"I, for one, have had about all the being social I can stand for one year," Stevie declared.

"Tell us about the wedding," Carole urged her. "Was the bride's dress to die for?"

Lisa settled herself in Carole's window seat. "Go on, Stevie. Give us all the details."

"I have to admit, it was pretty cool. Robin's parents pulled out all the stops. The place was filled with flowers, especially yellow roses, which were the bride's favorite."

"What about the dress?" Carole prodded.

"My dress was very nice, thanks. Kind of a summery floral patterned vest with a knee-length pleated skirt. My mom even loaned me her pearls."

"Not *your* dress!" Carole yelled. "The bride's dress!"

"All right, all right," Stevie chuckled. "It was white."

Lisa rolled her eyes. "Duh."

"The top was lace with long sleeves that dipped below her wrists, and the back of it was cut really low, with four strands of pearls draped across."

Carole raised her eyebrows. "Sounds very sophisticated."

Stevie nodded. "The skirt was satin and kind of bell-shaped, but it had this huge train in the back."

"I definitely want a long train and veil when I get married," Lisa declared.

Stevie frowned. "That could be a problem."

"Why?"

"Who's going to want to marry you?" Stevie replied, struggling to keep a straight face.

"Oh, thanks a lot!" Lisa laughed.

"Maybe if you kept the veil over your face."

Lisa threw a little stuffed pony at her.

"Hey, careful with that!" Mrs. Devine had sent it home for Stevie. It was like the ones she had made for Carole and Lisa.

"I almost left out the best part," Stevie told them when they had all stopped giggling. "The bride and groom rode away in a horse-drawn carriage!"

"You're kidding!" Carole squealed. "What a great idea!"

"Dava didn't think so," Stevie said gleefully. "She spent the rest of the party telling anyone who would listen how a white stretch limo would have been so much more chic. After a while her mother got fed up and told her to be quiet or she would have to leave the party."

"How wonderful," Carole said.

"It sounds to me like you had plenty of adventures

of your own while you were gone," Lisa declared. "You attended the social event of the Massachusetts season, saved a horse's life, and ruined an outfit you hated. So the visit wasn't a complete washout."

"How did your mom take it when she saw your clothes?" Carole asked Stevie.

"When she heard what had happened with Sugar, she was so proud that she didn't care at all," Stevie told her. "And the look on Dava's face when she saw Will with me was worth the whole trip."

Lisa sat up a little. "It turned out they knew each other?"

Stevie nodded with a satisfied grin. "Remember how I told you Dava had gone on a trail ride in order to impress a boy?"

Lisa and Carole nodded.

"Turns out that boy was Will!"

"You're kidding!"

Stevie held up her hands for silence. "I've saved the best part for last," she declared, pulling a folded piece of paper out of the pocket of her jeans. "This morning my dear cousin Dava sent me an e-mail."

Lisa grimaced. "Uh-oh. What mean things did she say this time?"

"Lisa," Stevie said in shocked tones, "you misjudge

Dava. She has nothing but nice things to say about me. According to this, she can't wait for me to come back."

"What?" Carole snatched the e-mail away. "What's up with that?"

"I wouldn't trust her for a minute," Lisa declared, running across the room to read over Carole's shoulder. "She must want something."

"You're absolutely right. Turns out she's desperate to get Will to like her and—get this—she wants me to send him an e-mail saying nice things about her!"

The three girls grew teary-eyed with laughter at the very idea.

"Of course you're not going to do it," Carole said.

"Actually I am."

Her two friends stopped laughing and stared at her.

"Why, Stevie?" Lisa demanded. "She was so mean to you!"

Stevie smiled slyly. "This way she'll never be able to hold it over my head that I didn't try to help. And I'm going to explain to Will why I'm saying such nice things."

Carole nodded. "Pretty smart."

"Thank you," Stevie said with grave dignity. "There's just one thing I need from the two of you."

"What's that?" Lisa asked.

"Some help composing my e-mail to Will. I have to

figure out something—anything—nice to say about my cousin."

Carole looked surprised. "What makes you think we'd be any good at that?"

"Well, my dear friends," said Stevie, "after all those whoppers you two wrote me while we were apart, I figure you're practically professional fiction writers by now!"

ABOUT THE AUTHOR

BONNIE BRYANT is the author of more than a hundred books about horses, including The Saddle Club series, The Saddle Club Super Editions, the Pony Tails series, and Pine Hollow, which follows the Saddle Club girls into their teens. She has also written novels and movie novelizations under her married name, B. B. Hiller.

Ms. Bryant began writing The Saddle Club in 1986. Although she had done some riding before that, she intensified her studies then and found herself learning right along with her characters Stevie, Carole, and Lisa. She claims that they are all much better riders than she is.

Ms. Bryant was born and raised in New York City. She still lives there, in Greenwich Village, with her two sons.

Don't miss the next exciting
Saddle Club adventure . . .

Stray Horse
Saddle Club #100

Something's wrong at home, and Lisa feels powerless
every time her parents get angry at her or at each
other. When CARL, the County Animal Rescue
League, puts out an SOS for volunteers, Lisa knows
she's found a place where she'll be appreciated. Before
long, a stray horse named PJ steals her heart. But just
as things seem to be getting better, Lisa's parents de-
liver some news that will change her life forever.

Stunned and upset, Lisa pulls away from everyone—
even her friends—and devotes herself to caring for PJ.
Stevie and Carole know that The Saddle Club can
pull through anything, as long as they're together. But
how can they help Lisa if she keeps shying away?
When a fiery and famous show jumping team arrives at
Pine Hollow and begins stirring up trouble, Carole and
Stevie have to convince Lisa that they need her
help—fast.

MEET
the SADDLE CLUB

Horse lover CAROLE . . .
Practical joker STEVIE . . .
Straight-A LISA . . .